The Lost Princess

by
Adina A. Lev

Order this book online at www.trafford.com
or email orders@trafford.com

Most Trafford titles are also available at major online book retailers.

Printed in Victoria, BC, Canada.

ISBN: 978-1-4269-1448-5 (soft cover)

Library of Congress Control Number: 2009932867

*Our mission is to efficiently provide the world's finest, most comprehensive book publishing
service, enabling every author to experience success. To find out how to publish your book, your
way, and have it available worldwide, visit us online at www.trafford.com*

Trafford rev. 12/28/09

www.trafford.com

North America & international
toll-free: 1 888 232 4444 (USA & Canada)
phone: 250 383 6864 ♦ fax: 812 355 4082

Preface

This book is an ENTIRE work of fiction. As with most books of fantasy, romance and intrigue, MANY (most) of the references here are purely from my imagination.

I do NOT know if the Prince of Wales has any illegitimate children and I am not suggesting he does. It just makes for an interesting story.

So, when you read this, PLEASE do not assume that there are any facts attributed to the Prince of Wales, his family or anything else. And if there is anything in this book that happens to be true- it is a coincidence.

Also, any good attorney will have gone over this to make sure that everyone knows it is a work of fiction.

Thanks!

Chapter 1

A sharp knock on the office door brought James' head up abruptly. He had left strict orders that he wasn't to be disturbed.

"Enter" was his sharp barked reply. He hated being interrupted before he was to give the weekly report to the head of Royal Security, also known as His Majesty the Prince.

The door opened and a young woman entered with a PDA in one hand and a look of concern on her face. Her body language spoke volumes.

"Sir, we have a situation." She went over to his desk and slid the PDA in front of him.

"This report was filed by the computer ten minutes ago. I verified that it isn't a glitch. A unit is already on the way to the address of the last confirmed location. I expect that to come in the next" she looked at her watch "2 minutes. I thought you should know that something is up."

Her ear unit flashed indicating that it was ringing. She touched it "Laraby-go. Got it. Stay on location and start a search. You know the drill. Call back in 5 minutes for an update. Out" She looked at the older man "Sir. The unit confirms that the princess is missing."

1

His annoyance was immediately replaced by alarm, his mind reeling with the possibilities. "Which one? I thought they were all at Highpoint for the family reunion."

"The other one, sir."

He picked up the phone "Get me Butler now." He hung Up the phone and looked at Laraby. "Get me the file so we can brief him. I also want the last Intel on my computer in the next…"

"It's already there. I thought Butler was on sabbatical?"

"He was. I think that this takes precedence over his needing a holiday."

"I don't think losing your wife in a skiing accident is taking a holiday, sir"

"Laraby, men like Butler will only sit and stew and eventually eat the end of their own guns if they aren't doing something. His wife's death is a tragedy. But if this is a move against the Royal family or could be a scandal, I need someone with Butler's talents to secure the situation. Get him in here, now."

James didn't need to yell- ever. The look in his pale blue eyes was enough to scare even the most stout of heart. It was one of the things that the Prince had liked about him, almost feared about him. James Bancroft was a man of many passions. And one of those passions was the protection of the Royal family. He had never married but was definitely a ladies' man. He had his share of lovers but he always made it clear that his first love was queen and country. He was often gone for days at a time ensuring that the security of the royals was impenetrable. The ones that were the most trouble were the royals themselves. Too many time he had to bail them out of problems that they created. This was one of them.

He looked up at Laraby. She was a pretty young thing. And one hell of an agent. She had worked her way up to be his right hand. She had graduated second in her class at Oxford, had immediately gone into Scotland Yard's organized crime unit and had been recruited by MI-6. In under ten years she had proven to be an excellent agent and almost intuitive to the director's mind.

They'd had a brief affair but it fizzled out almost as soon as it began. They were both too much alike, but they had become friends after a fashion. Once in a while, they shared each other's bed, but not often enough to become office gossip. And they both knew in their hearts that if it were necessary, they would both throw each other to the wolves to protect the Crown. It was that living on the edge that kept them from getting closer to each other.

"Laraby, you know this case as well as anyone. What is your risk estimation?"

"In my opinion, she should have been taken out of the equation years ago, possibly during infancy, then this would not be necessary."

"I agree. But the Queen is a stickler about murder and her son is very sentimental when it comes to his children, bastards or not."

A knock on the door interrupted their conversation.

"Enter" James called out

A dark head poked it's way in. "You wanted to see me?"

Surprise registered on James' face. "Butler, I thought you were still out. Come in and shut the door."

Butler stepped in, shut the door and stood there, sizing up the situation. "I came in to sign some papers up in personnel. Your secretary caught up with me on the fourth floor. Did you need something?"

"I'm very sorry about your wife. Katy was a very warm and caring person. It is always a tragedy when someone so young is lost to us."

Butler looked down for a moment, his every breath was an agony as he felt his heart thud in his chest, a stabbing pain that almost brought him to his knees. All he wanted to do was to go home and wallow in his pain. He lifted his head and choked back a sob. "Thank you, sir. It is hard, but we must carry on, that's what we are always told. Or some crap like that."

James nodded. This was definitely the person to handle the situation. "Butler, have a seat. We have a situation that I need you in on."

Butler walked over to the chair and folded his long frame into it. At six feet even, wiry and lean, he was very athletic. His work required that he stay fit.

"How well do you know of the heir a-parent's activities in the sixties?"

"Not much I'm afraid. He is older than me and we definitely didn't run in the same circles, if you know what I mean."

"O.K., history time. Back in sixty nine, the Prince wanted to go to the States and see what all of the fuss was about. The Queen and the consort thought that this wasn't a bad thing. He had just graduated from Oxford and was due for military service the coming fall. So they sent him over the pond with an entourage and an MI-6 detail. During that visit, they went to New York and lived the typical twenty-something night life. While there, the Prince fell in love with a local girl, a Maria Vasquez. He was madly in love with her, to the point that he refused to leave her at the end of his schedule. He began talking about abdication and marrying her.

Of course the Queen was beside herself and sent his father to talk some sense into the lad. Unfortunately, by the time this occurred the girl was in the family way and the Prince had no doubt that the child was his. He stayed on in New York until the child was born. The press had been told that he had extended his stay abroad to further his education. He had been given a year waiver in the military while he studied at Harvard. That was the official story. The MI-6 report was that the Prince refused to leave until his child was born, fearing that an accident would befall the child or it's mother."

"How far off the mark was he?"

"Not very. The orders had been given that once the Prince was safely away, that the woman would have a fall on the subway."

"Got it. So the Prince stayed on until the child was born and then came home."

"Right. As soon as the child was born, it was a Royal. The Prince had made sure that his name was in the appropriate box and a princess was born."

Butler sat back and furrowed his brow "It, or she rather, was allowed to live? I know that it sounds callous, but what was the Queen thinking?"

"She was thinking that the law was specific. And as yet, His Highness did not have any heirs and the way he was carrying on, it wasn't looking too likely that he was going to have any. An illegitimate can inherit the thrown if there are no legitimates to claim it. And as His Highness had announced that he was the father, the child was and is a princess with rights to the thrown."

"All of this is fascinating, but how is my help needed?"

"The princess is missing." James replied flatly

Butler sat up instantly and leaned forward. "How?" It was all business now, the pain in his chest forgotten for a time, replaced by a sense of threat and dread. Illegitimate or not, she was a Royal and it was his job to protect them.

James stood and walked over to a painting on the wall. He swung it away from the wall and punched the buttons on the keypad to the safe that the painting had been hiding. He opened the door, pulled out a file and closed the door again. It made a faint beep as the locks engaged and he replaced the painting. James walked back to his desk and sat down. Opening the file he pulled out some pictures and some sheets of paper and handed them to Butler.

Butler looked at each picture. It was of a woman in her late thirties to forties, pretty with dark hair, olive skin and a nice smile. One picture was of her and a couple of kids getting into a minivan. Another was of her in a suit arguing in what appeared to be in a courtroom. The last picture was of her sitting in her living room reading a book. The time stamp on the bottom of the pictures was two weeks old.

James continued "We keep a watch on her, checking on her daily. Mostly one of our units does a drive by of her and her family at random intervals. She, like the rest of the Royals has a location tag implanted in her person. Laraby, your turn."

Laraby stepped forward and clicked a remote to a screen behind the director. Immediately a computer display came up. "You can see here that at 0945 the princess's tag was working properly and giving her GPS location. It appears that she was on her way to work. She is an attorney with the prosecutor's office in Trenton, New Jersey. At 0947 her tag disappears from the tracker.

We immediately ran a diagnostic on the system and everything is operating normally. A unit was contacted and there was no electrical power surge or WMD to disrupt the signal. Her trail went cold three blocks from her office. Her car, also GPS enabled was found idling at a stop sign with no sign of her. The team checked her children, they are safe and in school. A unit has been placed with each child just in case this is an attack on the Royal family, but they are staying out of sight."

Again, Butler furrowed his brow. "Why weren't the children pulled out and put in a safe house?"

James sat back and gave a long sigh. "That my boy is because they don't know who or what their mother is. And neither does she, for that matter. It was felt by the Queen and the Prince that it would be better for all concerned that no one ever find out about her. At least not as long as the Prince was able to reproduce."

"I see. So if the Prince never had children, there was one in the wings, albeit a girl, but still one to carry on the family line."

"Right. And even a bastard can claim the thrown so long as the Prince had acknowledged her existence." James sat back and lifted one of the pictures of the princess. "She is pretty, intelligent and totally ignorant of who her father is. She had been told that he was a one night stand and her mother didn't remember his name. Chalk it up to the free love and hippie days of the sixties. Her name is Sara Cohen, she is an attorney and a mother of two and she is also a princess. Mr. Butler, I need you to go to the states and find her. As long as she is missing, her existence is a threat to the Crown. She can be held hostage, she can be used as blackmail material, she can also be used as a pawn. You must find her, dead or alive and bring her back. At all costs, Mr. Butler."

Chapter 2

Her head was throbbing. The last thing that she remembered was someone hitting her minivan from behind. She had rolled down her window when someone had sprayed her in the eyes with pepper spray. She vaguely remembered the shock that ran through her when she taser prongs were shot into her chest from the window opening. After that the room went black. Now she mentally took stock of her situation. She was blind folded and gagged. The gag tasted like adhesive, so she figured it was tape. Her hands were bound behind her in what felt like plastic tie wraps. She attempted to stretch out and felt resistance all around her.

Great. She was locked in a trunk. She could feel the vehicle moving. At least she could still hear. It sounded like street roads. There was no music coming from the main portion of the car.

It still had "new car" smell. New car smell. That meant that it was a mafia trunk. All new cars had a glow in the dark tag with instructions on how to pop the trunk from the inside. She had begun to call it a mafia trunk due to the reputed favorite mode of transport for mafia victims. She felt around with her hands behind her. Her hands found the flat wall that indicated the back seat. She tucked herself into a small ball and rolled over so that now her hands were facing the trunk opening. Feeling her way around, she found the tag and pulled it. She felt like cheering when she felt the cold air rush in. To her horror, the car screeched to a halt. Someone opened the driver door and got out. She felt more air rush in when the trunk lid was fully opened. She felt the sunlight hit her face. The next thing she new a cloth was being placed over her nose. Since tape was covering her mouth she had no choice but to inhale the sweet smelling fumes. She was surprised that the person holding the cloth hadn't said a word. That was the last thing to run through her mind.

Chapter 3

As the plane touched down, Butler gathered his gear into the small computer bag that he had brought with him. He really liked this new computer. It weighed about three pounds and could fit in a legal sized manila envelope. It came fully loaded and coupled with his flash drives, the memory was unbelievable. He had slept for a few hours then woke, ate his meal then reviewed the file on Sara Cohen.

She had been born Sara Vasquez in Brooklyn, New York. She was the oldest of four children. She had been raised by her mother and step father. Graduated high school then college. She went on to law school, passed the New York bar, married, moved to New Jersey and passed the bar in New Jersey. She went to work for the Prosecutor's Office, had two children of her own, girls. Her husband had a bad gambling problem and she divorced him after they had been forced to file for bankruptcy. A memo in the file said that he had been borrowing from loan sharks and was not a stranger to their collection practices. Neither Sara or children had seen him since she had divorced him five years previous. She was not involved with anyone at the time and led a very predictable life. Too predictable for Butler's liking.

She went to the gym after work every Tuesday and Thursday as well as an aerobics class on Sundays while the kids visited with their grandparents who had moved to New Jersey to be closer to their children who all had moved across the bridge.

Sara's sisters were all professionals. One sister was an architect, a brother who was a doctor and younger sister who was also a lawyer. Only two of the grown children had children of their own. All four were either divorced, married or living with someone. Everyone of those people had to be checked out. He made a list of things that could be handed off to the unit already in place.

The file that had been made by MI-6 had been beyond complete. It started with the day she had been born and the last entry had been made at the time of her disappearance. Butler read every word. By the time the plane had landed, he knew everything that there was to know about her. When she had started to walk, who her first grade teacher had been, who she dated, when she had started menstruation, even her deliveries of her children from the drugs she had been given to the time she had pushed each one out.

You had to hand it to MI-6, he thought. They were nothing if not thorough. Since the file was on a flash drive, it contained everything about her including pictures and her GPS implant tracking numbers. It was a little known fact that all of the royals had been implanted shortly after the devices became available. The devices were the size of a grain of rice and could be implanted anywhere with no anesthesia. It could even be done without the person being aware of it. Say the doctor wanted to do some dental work, while he was in there, he could in insert it in the soft tissue area of the jaw where it wouldn't be detected or if felt, could be explained away as some part of the bony structure that was changing with age. Most people don't really notice the bony structures inside of their mouths and after a few days, accept any changes as normal, especially if they aren't bothered by them as was the case of Sara.

He got off the plane and went through customs. Nothing to declare, security checked his bag and stamped his passport. The MI-6 unit met him a few feet further. Introductions were made all around and he was escorted to a big, black SUV. There he was given a 9mm Glock-24 and ammunition to go with it. The gun was so small and lightweight that his large hand swallowed it. He put it in the holster that he was given and slid it onto his belt. It fit nicely against his waist and was almost completely hidden by the "pancake" holster.

The leader of the Team, Tim Mack briefed him on the local elements and how they affected things.

Butler listened and took it all in, the whole time studying the Team members and the landscape through the SUV's tinted windows.

"A car is ready for you back at the building." Tim told him. "Here is a bank card and a credit card. Remember to get receipts for everything. Finance is a real stickler for these things."

He chuckled "Tell me about it. One time I had to get some ammunition from less than reputable sources. I included the information and the amount used in my report. Would you believe that Finance reported to D.I.A. that I might be less than honest in my amount expenditures?"

Tim nodded. "I believe it. Too bad it isn't like the films, unlimited budgets, no reports or Internal Affairs breathing down your neck. By the way, sorry about your wife. I was surprised that they pulled you off of bereavement leave."

Butler lowered his head for an instant, the pain a fresh stab in his heart. He looked up and out of the window to regain his composure. "Thank you. Small world we live in when you hear about her passing over here."

"The Team doesn't miss much there, mate. Still, I'm sorry. It hurts the hardest when it's someone your own age."

Butler just nodded. He took a deep breath. "Yeah. Tell me about it. Anyhow" he sniffed "the reason I'm here. Tell me what you've got, your thoughts and theories."

Tim gave a single nod then opened a brief case and pulled out a manila folder. "Sara Cohen is a prosecutor for the state of New Jersey. Her specialty is prosecuting gangs, namely 'The Bloods'. They are a notorious street gang, mainly black young men although they also recruit women. They are more formidable than the IRA ever was. They recruit elementary school children and on. Like the Italian mafia of the fifties and sixties, the U.S. today is seeing the same activities and development. And like in the fifties and sixties, the prosecutor's are going after the heads of the snake to try to keep a lid on the violence. That's where Sara comes in. She is the state's attorney general's favorite local pit bull. I've watched her in court. She is formidable and brilliant. Not to mention one heck of a looker in heels. She definitely took after her mother, ears and all."

That drew a chuckle out of everyone in the vehicle.

"That's one avenue of theory, that the Bloods have taken her out for their own protection. But this just came across our desk while you were airborne. I've already sent it to the chief." Tim handed him a picture. It was a picture of the oldest legitimate child of the Prince of Wales having sex with a young woman in a hotel room. The picture showed both of their faces clearly and it was definitely consensual from the look of pleasure on the girl's face. "she has been identified as an Al-Qaeda operative. How she got past security is beyond me, but whispers in the rumor mill are that the young Prince is not happy with the stand that England has taken siding with the U.S. and that when he secures the thrown, things are going to change."

"Are you serious?! Is he fucking daft?"

Tim shrugged "Just goes to show that when you think with the little head and not the big head, things can get buggered in an instant. So, the theories are: number one, that this is gang related and while our problem, can get sticky with the locals. Number two, that Al-Qaeda had found out about our lost princess and are going to use it as either black-mail material or are taking out any threats to the young Prince's ascension when grandma passes. You are aware that the Queen was diagnosed with an inoperable brain tumor two days ago?"

He nodded. "Yes. I also heard that there was a possibility that His Royal Highness was going to step aside to let the younger take over. This could definitely be used against him and his judgment."

"Or it could be a warning that they are going to take out all but the heir that they can count on. If they take out all of the heirs, legitimate or otherwise, England could be in one heck of a lot of trouble."

Butler shrugged "How could he get anything past parliament? It's not like the king can really do anything that the people are against?"

"Think about this Butler. Are the people really in favor of going against Al-Qaeda? I've been listening to the rumbles out in the fields. I got back from a brief taste of Iraq a few weeks ago and the Brits there aren't so sure that we should be fighting with the Yanks, that the U.S. has lost focus and are just sitting there trying to get rid of all of their old ammo at the cost of the soldiers that aren't even part of the U.S. If we had a king on the throne that felt that we shouldn't be there, how long would parliament last if they voted against him? Not too long, I would wager. And, we're here."

Chapter 4

"I WANT ANSWERS NOW GODDAMMIT!!!" then the phone being thrown at the wall was all the sound that echoed through the Prosecutor's Office. Everyone stopped what they were doing and stared at the door of the Chief Prosecutor's office. All that could be heard was the humming of the computers and the ringing phones.

The elevator chime was like a shot from a starter's pistol, everyone hurrying to move. The door slammed open and the Chief came barreling out of the office. His rage and his energy was palpable to those around him. He charged to the elevator door and punched the button. As the doors opened, he nearly collided with the Chief of Trenton Police Department.

"About fucking time, Mike. What the hell took you so long?!"

"Pete, calm down before you have a heart attack. I've got every cop on the street going door to door and building to building. The street camera's are being reviewed right now and every snitch that ever was is being rousted right now. Anything that can be done is being done. We have the Feds from the city in our computer room right now. No one is laying down on this."

"Follow me" he barked and turned on his heel. He walked into his office and went over to the phone that he threw. Mike shut the door quietly behind them.

Pete sat at his desk and looked at the clock. He wiped his face with his hands while he collected his thoughts.

"O.K., I'm calm. What have you got?"

"Sara's car is seen turning onto South Broad and going into the alley way towards that parking garage. The camera's don't pick up anything after that. Several cars and vans are seen leaving the garage and the alley way. We're i.d.ing the plates now and running them as fast as we can."

"What about the cameras from the jail out back?"

"Since the jail was closed, those camera's have been deactivated, so nothing there."

"This is fucking wonderful. Sara was supposed to give closing arguments today in about one hour. Her second chair is up to speed, but we need this like a hole in the head. Mike, I don't need to tell you what will happen to this case against Borden if Sara doesn't show. Or worse, if she's killed and we link it to the Bloods. We had to sequester the jury because of threats. If word gets out that she is missing- the asshole will walk."

The Chief stood up and walked over to the window and looked out at downtown Trenton. Hard to believe that this was the capital city. The place was an eye-sore for the state of New Jersey. Between the pollution, the gangs and the out of control taxes, people were leaving in droves. He turned back to the top lawyer and shook his head.

"Pete, I'm not going to blow sunshine up your skirt. It doesn't look good. CSI found pepper spray on the driver's side window. From all appearances, it looks like Sara got hit from behind by another car. Since it was bumper to bumper, there isn't much trace. She probably rolled down the window far enough to exchange data, got sprayed and the perp was able to gain entry through the partially rolled down window. CSI thinks that he used a taser to gain control of her. Something about the electrical current reacting with the pepper spray and leaving some type of trace. They also found a small amount of blood on the steering wheel. Not enough to suggest anything lethal, but enough to attract attention. Have you called your wife yet?"

He shook his head "Not yet, but that's what I have to do once you walk out of here. I thought things were tough being married to the lead defense in this case and having my sister-in-law as lead prosecutor, now I have to tell my wife that her big sister is missing and that her client is probably behind it. I wish to God that the judge had allowed Amanda to recuse herself."

Chapter 5

S he opened up her eyes and waited while they adjusted to the dim light around her. Her hands and feet were free and the tape had been taken off of her mouth. Feeling her wrist for her watch she felt a small dismay that it was gone. Well, so much for knowing how long she had been unconscious and missing.

She had to pee like everything. As her eyes adjusted, she saw a small toilet in one corner. Carefully she walked over to it and found that it was a type of port-a-potty that they use in hospitals. She checked it out. No booby traps or anything on it, but she wasn't taking a chance. She squatted over it, making sure that she didn't touch the surface in case there had been something on it. She felt herself and was satisfied that she hadn't been assaulted while she had been unconscious. That was one small comfort.

After she finished relieving herself, she found an unopened box of tissue on the floor next to the toilet. At least she didn't have to drip dry. When that was done, she adjusted her skirt and walked back to the small cot that she had been laying on.

She sat in the dim light and gathered information. Her stepfather had been a POW in Vietnam. One of the things he said was that you always take stock of the situation so that you know what you have at your disposal should the opportunity to escape present itself.

Looking around, she began to take stock. The room was being lit by a small night light next to the door. She quietly got off the cot to checked it out. It had a dimmer on it. She adjusted the dimmer and it got brighter, but not by a lot. Maybe enough to read by if you sat close enough, but that was about it.

It was a small windowless room about ten by ten. The door was wood and was double bolted. She checked and found it locked. No such luck Sara, she thought. There was a small slot hinged to the bottom of the door. She assumed that was where her captor would slide food in. So, she was going to be kept alive and comfortable for a while. But who knew how long. And since she hadn't seen who took her, the odds of being killed were going down. It was some small comfort.

There was a light weight blanket but the room was warm enough. On the floor next to the cot was a bible. She picked it up. Soft cover. No help there. Lots of small sticky tabs highlighting different passages. That was something to think about.

She checked the toilet again. It was bolted to the floor and all of the screws had been replaced by rivets. Breaking it apart to use as a weapon was useless. She heard a soft scuffling at the door. The slot opened and a burger and fries with a bottle of water were shoved through. The flap closed immediately and the sound of the locking mechanism sliding back into place was the scuffling noise that Sara had heard. Her stomach rumbled as the smell of the burger wafted through the air. She had no idea how long she had been there but she barely had time for anything for breakfast except the granola bar she had eaten from the emergency stash of food in the car.

Her mind leaped forward. The kids. She had made arrangements for her next door neighbor to make sure they got off of the bus. Her oldest was fifteen and quite capable of watching her younger sister for a few hours. But, if she didn't call around six, she would get worried and try her cell phone.

She absently patted her pockets in case that got over looked. Nope, empty, everything gone. So were her shoes and her jewelry. As she was feeling her pockets on her blouse she noticed that her bra felt looser. She nearly choked as she felt her bra and found that the under wires had been taken out. The mother fucker had her naked or nearly naked at one point! Then dressed her again. She hoped that when this was all over that she would get the chance to punch him or them square in the face.

Her mind went back to the kids. Someone should have noticed she was missing by now. Damn! She thought, the trial. Today was closing arguments and she wasn't there. Phil had second chair and was quite capable of filling in. He wasn't as expressive as she was, he didn't have quite the flair for theatrics, but he could get the point across to the dullest of bricks, so he would close well. The trial was a slam dunk. The defense had put up a good fight, but all in all, Sara knew she had won. This was all she needed, though.

Early on they had sequestered the jury after one of them had received a letter in the mail with pictures of their kids and their pets. After that, a new jury had been chosen and all of them sequestered from day one. They were hearing the trial from a closed room and pretty much watching it on TV.

Amanda had protested that this was unconstitutional, that the accused had the right to meet the jury. Sara had agreed and put the jury in with twenty other people, introduced each one with another's name so that even if one of the members of the Blood's had gotten the list, they wouldn't know which ones were jurists and which ones were fill ins. After that, the jurists had been placed in a room to watch the trial on closed circuit TV., had gotten on the bus in the cover of darkness and were kept in a different hotel each night. Sara was not taking any chances. Danny Borden had personally executed a three year old girl in front of her father after the father had burned him for drug money. Then Borden proceeded to dissect the man's baby's momma in front of him. The woman survived only to be shot in front of the courthouse the day she was to give her testimony to the grand jury. Borden was linked to more than a dozen hits that he either ordered or had a direct hand in. This guy was a monster and Sara was heading the team that was going to put him away for the rest of his life. Too bad that New Jersey had repealed the death penalty. If anyone deserved it or had earned it, it was Hakiem Borden.

She knew that when she didn't show in court, Amanda would demand to know why, both professionally and personally. Then they would all call her mother and after that a circus would ensue. Mom and Dad would take the kids to their house and Amanda would be up Pete's ass to find her.

Sara just wished that there was some way she could let her family know that she was all right. She opened the burger and checked for pills or something else. Nothing. The bottle of water didn't look as if it had been tampered with. Same for the fries. She ate and went to the bathroom again. She laid down and tried to sleep. Better get some rest while you can, she thought. Things were definitely going to get interesting.

Chapter 6

_____

Amanda looked over at the Prosecutions table and was puzzled. Usually her anal retentive, always punctual sister was in her seat half hour before everyone else. Amanda tapped her finger on the note pad that she kept between her and her client. The guy was a first rate sleaze ball not to mention guilty as hell. But it was her solemn oath to defend her clients passionately and without prejudice. Up until now, that hadn't been a problem. And she knew that she should have recused herself. But there was something in her ego that wouldn't let her bow out of this one. Going toe to toe with Sara was the ultimate. It had led to many interesting conversations at family gatherings. When Sara had first approached the judge that there may be a conflict of interests between the two attorneys, Amanda had been vehement in her argument that she could see past their personal issues and relationships and would not have a problem proving that her client was innocent of the allegations. The judge had smirked and said if Amanda didn't have a problem and the client didn't have a problem then neither did he.

At first it was funny that they would finally be pitted against each other in the court room. Sara had never tried to take her on before. Even as kids, Sara had always been the peace maker except when it really mattered to her, then she would let her true colors show. Amanda always had admired that in her sister, even when it was directed at her. They had both expressed concern when the first jury had been dismissed and the new jury had been chosen. Both had gone for the jugular when Sara had pulled the whole jury parade. The younger sister silently applauding her sister's initiative the whole time she argued about it's constitutionality. And now on the day of closing arguments, Sara wasn't at her usual perch, giving her that small smile she made whenever she thought that she had won. Well not this time big sister. This time, she was the one who was going to win.

The judge entered and the Deputy Sheriff called all to rise and be heard. As they all sat after the judge had gotten settled, the Prosecutor second chair, Phil Wilke stood and cleared his throat.

"Your Honor, due to some unforeseen circumstances, I will be handling closing for Prosecutor Cohen."

Judge Cutter looked over his glasses "Well, since you've been sitting second chair all this time, carry on young man."

At that moment, Amanda's assistant came into the room, closely followed by Amanda's husband.

"Your Honor" Pete began "I beg your pardon your honor, may I approach the bench?"

"Prosecutor Inverso, please by all means, approach."

"Your Honor, the two attorneys should also be part of this."

Judge Cutter pulled off his glasses, "Well, the more the merrier." He motioned them all to gather.

"Thank you, your Honor. I am going to make a motion for a continuance on behalf of both parties. Prosecutor Cohen is missing and all indications say that she has been abducted."

Amanda felt like she had been gut-punched. "Pete, please tell me that this is some horrible joke."

He shook his head "Her car was found in the alley behind the court house running and the door was left open. There is also evidence of pepper spray and taser usage. And given the history of this case, we have reason to believe that the accused or associates of the accused may have had something to do with this."

Amanda looked over at her client. Her blood ran cold. He was sitting there smug as ever and the look he gave her was that of a predator that had just eaten a big meal.

She looked back at the judge. "Your Honor, I don't believe that a continuance is necessary and by postponing the closing arguments, it is just delaying the inevitable acquittal of my client."

A bomb could have gone off in the room and no one could have been more surprised at that moment. Pete looked at his wife as if she had lost her mind. "Amanda, do you not understand that the man you are defending could have very well orchestrated your sisters abduction?"

"Yes, Pete, I do. I also understand that you and Sara would make the same objections had rolls been reversed."

"Man, I'm glad I'm not in either of your shoes" the judge commented. "Step back."

"Members of the jury" the judge began "Due to circumstances not relevant to this trial but directly affected by it, we will be taking a twenty four hour recess. You are to return to your housing locations and not talk about this trial. I do apologize for this delay. Court is dismissed and we will reconvene tomorrow morning at nine come hell or high water, is that understood Prosecutor Inverso?"

"Yes, your Honor. Thank you."

Amanda went back to her table and sat down. She sat there for a moment collecting her thoughts and trying to get her emotions in check. She put her tablet in her bag while

Borden sat there silent. Gone was the smug look. He actually looked concerned.

The court room emptied of everyone but the deputy sheriff and two of Borden's thugs. They looked respectable enough, in suits. But these same thugs had come by her office with Borden. They gave her the creeps. But her firm was making a ton of money on this client. It was also a chance for her to make a little cushion so that the firm could do more pro bono work. There were days when she asked herself if it was worth it. This was one of those times. She stood up, Borden along with her. He towered over her. He was muscular, tall and very intimidating. But Amanda was every inch the rabid terrier when she wanted to be. "Come with me, we need to talk. And leave your posse at the door."

She walked out of the court room and toward the lawyer's rooms. The two thugs took a seat at the door while she and Borden went into the room.

Amanda sat down and motioned for Borden to do the same.

He sat down and loosened his tie "I hate these monkey suits. I don't know how you can wear them all of the time. So, what's the delay for?"

Amanda calmly stood up and sat on the edge of the table so that she was eye to eye with the Blood's leader. She got her face so close to his that she could smell his after shave and see the small whole in his cheek left from a bout of chicken pox. "Hakiem, I want you to look me in the eye and swear on the life of your child that you had nothing to do with the disappearance of my sister."

He flinched back. "What the fuck are you talking about?"

"Prosecutor Cohen is missing. And it's just a coincidence that it is on the day of closing arguments."

"Look lady. I respect you and from where I was sitting, it looks like I am gonna walk on this. That's why I paid you the big bucks. And true as that, you made me look like a young upstanding citizen. Why would I screw that up by taking out the competition? If I was gonna roll like that, it would have been during the trial, not the last day of it. I'm tellin' you, you got the wrong idea."

She sat down in the chair at the head of the table and looked at him. "Here is where you stand. The head Prosecutor is missing and presumed abducted. You say that you have nothing to do with it. By the time we go back into the court room tomorrow, the jury is going to know about it one way or another. That is definitely going to work against us, especially the way this trial has been running. That will be your built in grounds for appeal. God forbid we should need it."

He grabbed her arm and pressed down hard against the table "What do you mean grounds for appeal? I'm telling you that we're going to win this."

She looked down at his arm and pulled hers from under his. She knew that the panic button was only an inch from her hand. If she needed to, she'd push it in a heartbeat. "I suggest you keep your hands off of me. What I'm saying is that I have discredited every one of their witnesses and so far we haven't had any surprises come out of the woodwork. But depending on how the press spins this, you could go from a choir boy to looking like a guilty man just from circumstances that are beyond you control. It would help to no end if my sister were found.

"Now, just because I don't like surprises, if the jury comes back with a guilty verdict I am going to move for a mistrial due to prejudicing of the jury caused by the disappearance of the prosecutor and the press' contamination of the jury. I will also ask that your bail be continued as the circumstances of your first trial haven't changed."

"You saying I could be going back to county lock-up?! BITCH! THAT AIN'T GONNA HAPPEN!"

He raised his hand to hit her. She fell back in the chair so hard that it flipped over backward, she jumped up and landed on her feet and landed a round house kick directly to his face. As he went down, she pushed the panic button. A second later two deputies were in the room and had Borden against the wall and were cuffing him. Pete was right behind them. As the deputies had Borden against the wall, Pete came up behind him and grabbed the thugs' head and rammed it against the muted beige wall.

"You don't fuck with my wife, you piece of shit!" he growled into the man's ear. Pete looked over at Amanda. "You all right, Baby?"

She nodded her head, slightly breathless. "You need to let go of my client. I'm not pressing charges. It was all a misunderstanding, but I think Mr. Borden and I have it all straightened out. Wouldn't you agree, Mr. Borden?"

"Yeah, what ever." He rasped out of the side of his mouth, since Pete still had his head pinned against the wall. Pete looked at her for the second time in an hour like she had lost her mind.

"Manda, are for fucking real? You hit the panic button. What, was that for kicks?"

"No sir. Like I said, it was a misunderstanding."

Pete shook his head. "You heard the lady. Un-cuff him. I'll have a deputy standing outside the door if there are any more 'misunderstandings'.

"Thank you, but I don't think that will be necessary, do you Mr. Borden?"

Hakiem rubbed his wrists as the deputy uncuffed him "No ma'am. I think we will be getting along just fine."

With that, the deputies left followed by Pete, but not before he whispered in Amanda's ear "this piece of shit had better be worth it."

Amanda watched the door close and picked up the overturned chair. "Now would you like to finish this briefing or would you just like to see everything unfold in the court room?"

Chapter 7

Butler checked out his room and tried the bed. The Team had a house, a "Brownstone" as they called it- in the City. It was four levels including the basement that housed the Team's operations department. All of the weapons and computer gear were there. The basement had been reinforced and self contained, so that in the event of a break in, war or terrorist attack, the room would be a safe haven. It also sported a full clinic, complete with an x-ray machine. The other three levels were for surveillance and the living area for the Team. Each member of the team was assigned for a two year posting. Any longer than that and the subject may become suspicious. The princess wasn't the only person that the Unit was keeping tabs on. Certain delegates and operatives also needed them. The Team also provided security for the families of the delegates and ambassadors. Anytime that a British citizen needed something from home by the way of security the Team was in charge of it.

He looked over the briefing material that the Team had on hand. Even the highest ranking member of the team was in the dark as to the princess's identity. As far as they knew, she was a person of interest and that was all they needed to know. As far as Butler was able to determine, he was one of less than a dozen people who knew of her existence as a member of the Royal family. The fewer that knew, the better.

Looking at his watch, he left his bag on the bed, checked that his weapon in the shoulder holster was secured and left the room. He had left the briefing folder at the Director's office. No sense in letting a secret out, even amongst his comrades. You never knew who you could trust. He'd seen mothers sell out their own children to save their own lives. In all of the training he had been through, the one constant that he knew was that everyone had their price, you just had to find it. And it wasn't always money. Sometimes it was just to stop the pain that was being inflicted on the body or the mind. Terrorist didn't usually play nice.

Ten minutes after he had arrived at the base house, he was heading out to the SUV to go to the crime seen. Although anything that could have been gathered as evidence was already uploaded into the computer, there was something about actually being their that couldn't be captured on film.

It was getting dark fast and traffic was thinning out as the commuters had already left and the last of the turnpike regulars were hitting their exits after their long day at work.

Butler always thought that the highways here and at home weren't too different from each other. Lots of people leaving their little cubbies in some faceless, soulless building to drive home jammed next to other cars filled with nameless people all doing the same routines. Get up, go to work, toil for eight hours then drive home again, eat, sleep and get up to do it all over again. Never really knowing those around them, never really making a connection.

He shook his head to clear the maudlin mood that was descending on him. He had been half listening to Tim. The American football, while still not as exciting as European football, had wormed it's way into English sports bars. And since the Yanks had played a game in Great Britain, the fever was contagious. The game playing over there had been a ploy in order to cover a larger operation between the U.S. and Great Britain. A great number of suspected terrorist had to be moved out of England to be transported to Guantanamo Bay for interrogation. The number had been large enough to bring attention to the move, so a game had been devised as a cover. It had worked better than expected. England had been able to move the nastiest of their detainees and nearly empty the detention centers. And none the wiser. It had been brilliant. Not so this case, he thought. Something told his gut that this was going to get interesting and not in a good way.

Chapter 8

Amanda pulled up to her sister's house. The place was practically surrounded by cars. She counted no less than three uniformed cars, two unmarked cars, an SUV with state government plates, not to mention the cars belonging to all of her siblings, her parents, her husband and her aunts and uncles, her cousins and some friends. Good thing it was a warm night. The place was large, but family gatherings for the Cohen/Vasquez family were often overwhelming. Coupled with a family emergency, this was going to get real ugly real fast.

Amanda found a place to park the next block down and took the time walking to gather her courage. She was going to need every last bit of it. Here she was defending public enemy number one, the most likely suspect behind her older sister's disappearance and she wasn't backing down. She climbed the five stairs of the porch, held the doorknob and took a deep breath. Maybe she wouldn't be seen, what with all of those people here.

She opened the door and it was like a clap of thunder the way every sound in the room stopped and every eye was on her as she entered. For a second everyone just stood there, silently looking at her. A pin hitting the floor would have been

31

heard. For just a second. Then the room went back into a crazy frenzy. Wires were being strung to phone lines, to computers, to various recording devices. The ceiling fans were on full blast and every window had been opened to increase the circulation of air.

Amanda made her way to the living room. It was also packed with cops talking to every member of her family. It was here that she knew she couldn't escape. Every one stopped talking as her father and mother got up from the couch, staring at her. Sara's daughters had slid off of their grand parents' laps and sat in the vacated seats. This was the moment that Amanda had dreaded.

Her parents waded through the throng of family members and stood in front of their youngest daughter, the pain was etched on her mother's face. Coupled by the fear that they were all feeling, Amanda almost turned to run-almost.

They stood before her, hands joined. They had been married for thirty six years. They had weathered the best and the worst that life could throw at you together and were strongest when they were with each other. As long as they had each other, there wasn't anything that they couldn't overcome. So together they stood before their daughter.

It was her father who spoke first. "Amanda, you have got a hell of a lot of explaining to do." Barry Cohen was quiet. It was when he was quiet that his daughters had learned he was beyond angry. Even though they could count on one hand the times he had ever hit them, he could emanate rage like no one else. It was almost a tangible thing. And this was definitely one of those times.

"Dad, Mom….seriously, what was I supposed to do? What would Sara do?" Turning to her sister-in-law "Lisa, you're an attorney. What would you have done? Everyone here has decided that Borden and the Bloods are behind this without thinking it through. Why would he have her abducted the day of closing statements? As it stands, we had this won…"

"Like hell you did" her husband interrupted.

"Pete, your case was falling apart when that kid refused to testify against Borden. Every thing you had was circumstantial not to mention that Borden had an airtight alibi during the murders. You had no proof that he either ordered a hit or pulled the trigger himself. We had this one. So his taking Sara wasn't going to do him any good. If anything it is going to cost him, since I'm sure that the jury has gotten wind of the abduction by now. God only knows how the press is going to spin this."

"Dammit, Amanda. That piece of shit attacked you in the conference room!"

It was her mother's turn at her "He attacked you and you're still defending him? Are you stupido or loco?" Whenever her mother was upset, she lapsed into Spanglish.

"I'm neither one, Ma. What I am doing is defending my client. And he never laid a hand on me. I hit him with a round house kick and pushed the panic button. You should have seen Pete. I thought he was going to turn into the incredible hulk."

Pete blushed with anger and frustration. He loved this woman to death, but there were times that he questioned her sanity. Not too mention her warped sense of humor.

"You know, "Manda. There are times that I want to strangle you. And this is one of them. What if there hadn't been a panic button. What if he had gotten a hold of you? You ever think of that?"

She walked past her parents, weeded her way through her relatives, past her in-laws and went to her husband who was standing against the fire place mantle. She put her arms around him and hugged fiercely. "I know. But I am fine. I am also doing my job. Just like you do." Turning back to her parents she pulled Pete's arms around her.

"I'm sure that Borden isn't behind this. He was too shocked and if he had been behind it, she would have been back by now when I explained to him that the longer she is gone, the more likely the jury is going to think he is connected. And God forbid, anything happens to her, they will more than likely convict him not on evidence, but on the fact that the lead prosecuting attorney had been taken out by his crew and that he would be spending the rest of his life behind bars just for that." Shaking her head "He didn't do it, or she would be home by now."

A man in a suit cleared his throat to get their attention "She's right. Everyone on the street, every informant that we have says the same thing. This wasn't gang related. The Crips even said the same thing. As much as they would like to see Borden off the streets, this isn't his work. If you take out someone big, like a prosecutor, all deals are off and the gangs begin spending more money getting out of jail than doing what they like to do. It's bad for business. Same reason the mob doesn't go after prosecutors without facing huge reprisals from their own people. I'm Agent Sexton with the FBI. I'll be the lead on this." He shook hands with Sara's parents and with Pete then Amanda.

Nodding to the rest of the clan assembled, he continued. "Most of these cases, the abductor is someone the victim knew. With that in mind, does anyone know the whereabouts of Ms. Cohen's ex-husband?"

Around the room, everyone looked at each other and shook their heads.

Barry looked to his wife and shrugged. "The last time that any of us saw him was the day the divorce was final and we all gathered here to celebrate."

His wife, Maria, lightly slapped her husband's chest. "Barry, that's awful. You don't celebrate a divorce. Lightly applaud, but not celebrate." She turned to the family and made waving motions. The crowd parted and seats were vacated for the parents and the agent. Maria made a seating gesture for him and took her own seat. Her granddaughter, Theresa Josephine, or T.J., resettled on her grandmother's lap. She was eight and small for her age. She was Sara's youngest child and therefore doted on by her mother and older sister, 15 year old Cassidy.

Maria tucked the little girl's head under her chin and absently rocked her. "Agent, my family wasn't happy about Sara's marrying Kurt Peterson. We made no secret about it. It was a well known fact that he was a gambler and not a very good one. But Sara was in love with him and they eloped shortly after she passed the bar. They had the girls, but about the time that Theresa here turned two, Kurt's gambling had forced the family into bankruptcy. For a few months there, they had to live with us. One day, some knee breakers for a loan shark came knocking on the door looking for Kurt. I had thought he was at work. They said to tell him that the boss wanted his money and they told me that he was in for fifty thousand. Fifty grand. I couldn't believe it. Then one of them said something about the boss told them that he would take a pretty little girl for trade. That was the final straw. I called the family and we got the money together. We also told Sara that she was welcomed to stay, but if she didn't put Kurt out, we were going to file for custody just for the girls' safety.

Sara finally opened her eyes and saw that this was not the way to live her life. That the girls were more important than the loser she was with. She kicked him out that day.

Thankfully she was already with the prosecutor's office and was able to keep her job. Six months later, the divorce was final and we haven't seen him since. He never paid child support, sent a birthday card to the girls or even just called to see how they were.

So, to answer your question Agent. We haven't seen Kurt in six years, and the better for it if you ask me. You don't think Kurt's behind this, do you? Not after all this time? He never objected to the divorce. He said he understood that his problem, his addiction was putting the girls and Sara in danger."

The agent looked up from his notebook. "Mrs. Cohen, I don't know anything for certain. What I do know is that statistically, the abductor has usually had some sort of contact with the victim, one way or another. What I do need from everyone in this room is a list of people that may have a grudge against you or someone in this family that you may know of. Also, has Sara reported anything weird, like someone following her or meeting the same person out of the blue recently. What may seem like something unimportant to you, sometimes means the most to us."

Chapter 9

On the other side of town, Butler was coming to the same conclusion. It had to be someone that knew Sara's routine, that had been watching her closely enough to know the best spot to grab her, but could be unnoticed by the general populace.

They were back in the SUV looking at computer pictures of the car and the street where Sara had been abducted. "Tim-Mrs. Cohen's ex. Where is he, these days? The file doesn't have anything updating him since the divorce was final."

Tim nodded. "Yeah. I know. We have a crew working on that. He dropped off the face of the planet a few weeks after the final papers came though. It was a unanimous decision that the loan sharks had taken him out. No activity on his credit cards, through the banks, nothing. Like I said, he dropped off the face of the earth."

Butler shook his head. "I don't buy it. Too convenient. Follow up on this again. And be careful. If I'm tugging this line, the Feds will be too. You can let them do most of the leg work. If they come up dry or are heading in a different direction, pick up where they fail. I want this guy run to the ground. If he did get whacked, find out who did it."

He went back to the computer screen and studied the pictures more closely. The Yanks' CSI people were good. Almost as good as his team. But the Team had other toys and gadgets that made their Intel a bit better. He zoomed in on a picture that was taken at the stop light just outside of the parking area that Sara had been heading for. Frame by frame it showed each car as it left. License plates were being checked and drivers investigated even as they sat there. Butler backed up a frame and looked closely at the picture "Bloody Hell! Tim! Look at this picture, look at the driver. Who is that?"

Tim looked at the computer screen and a look of disbelief ran across his face "Fuck me...that's Kang Cho. I thought he was in custody down in Cuba."

"Yeah, that's what I thought, too. Let's get back to the house. Someone has got a lot of explaining to do."

Chapter 10

Sara bolted upright on her small cot. Someone had been in the room with her. She was sure of it. She was a heavy sleeper, but not that heavy. She could still smell a man's after shave hanging in the air. She had felt a hand run over her hair. There must have been something in the food. Or even in the room. With so many drugs and chemicals out there, who could be sure. After all, when the kidnapper had stopped the car while she had been in the trunk, he had used chloroform on her. And this was a small room. It wouldn't take much to pipe it into the room to knock her out. She did a random check. Bra, panties and everything else seemed undisturbed. She was getting really freaked out that someone was fondling her while she was unaware. Getting off the cot, she walked to the door and tried the knob. Thing was locked tighter than a drum.

She turned the light on to it's brightest setting, which wasn't much. After relieving herself in the port-a-potty, she noticed that it had been emptied. So, she had been knocked out. Well, there went eating and drinking for a while. Picking up the bible, she opened it to the first tabbed passage. Genesis 3:1, and God put Adam in a deep sleep" so, this perv wants me to read about Adam and Eve. The next passage was about

Abraham and Sarah then Lot and his wife and her death. As Sara skimmed each passage, a pattern began to emerge.

"That mother fucking son of a bitch! Kurt, you mother fucker, let me out of here!"

She got up and threw the bible on the floor and began to beat on the door.

"You fucking son of a bitch. Let me out of here. Have you lost your mind? You kidnapped me so that I could be a dutiful wife? Have you have completely lost your mind? Let me out of here, now!"

She kept pounding at the door, alternately kicking it with her feet until they hurt too much. After a few more minutes she stopped. She wasn't making any headway except for hurting herself.

She went over and stood by the cot. This ass hole was dead meat. She began to look harder. The cot! That was it. She ripped the thin mattress to the floor and began to take the bed apart. Springs were what held the legs up when the cot was folded. She detached the springs and straightened the ends so that she could pick the lock. One of the things that she had mastered was lock picking. It was a skill she proudly possessed and had come in handy on more than one occasion. As she felt the lock begin to give, she became aware of a sweet odor in the room along with a fine mist that was being sprayed through the ceiling. Holding her breath, she jimmied the lock some more. Just as the door opened, her head began to swim and then things faded to black.

Chapter 11

The press was out in force. Sara's parents had taken the girls home with them while Sara's house was being held as "Command Central". The phones were tapped and ready to trace, computers were up and running, waiting for anything. Another computer was running probabilities of locations and hideouts for anyone with a tie to the Bloods. No house was being left untouched while Sara was missing. Amanda had gone home with Pete to shower and get ready for work.

The FBI had also sent their task force to help out, but until a call or some sort of ransom demand was received, there wasn't much to go on. The CSI unit had turned the car inside out. Nothing had yet turned up, but unlike those crime dramas on TV., things like this took time.

Amanda finished in the shower and turned the water off. She pulled back the curtain and grabbed the towel from the bar. The bar fell from the wall and for the billionth time she told herself that she or Pete would fix it this weekend.

Unfortunately, the weekends were always packed with family stuff, work, political obligations. Good thing we don't have kids she thought, how the hell would we find time to feed them, much less anything else. She put the towel bar back between the two arms that supported it and finished drying off. After running a brush through her hair and throwing on her makeup, she brushed past Pete who had his phone pressed to his ear. It was his turn in the small bathroom.

Another thing on the to do list, have the bathroom renovated and enlarged. Pete had worked his way through law school by doing construction. It wasn't that he couldn't do it, but he didn't have the time.

"Look, I'll be at the courthouse in an hour, get ready to close. I don't want this slime ball on the streets, not even for a second. Bye" Pete closed his phone and gave Amanda a hard look. "I don't even want to talk about it. And as long as Sara is missing, I don't even want to talk to you."

Amanda stood up from putting on her socks. She was already half dressed in her power suit and was getting her shoes on. "Pete, I'm telling you that Borden had nothing to do with this. I know that and you know that. They aren't organized enough to pull something like this off. And from what I've heard from the news, the gang task forces have made over a hundred arrests for other crimes that the Bloods have been accused of. Carly called to tell me that the phone has been ringing off the hook with new clients. I think all of you guys are looking in the wrong direction."

Pete had stopped shaving mid stroke to listen to her. "Then where should we be looking?"

She shrugged as she stepped into her shoes and adjusted her pants "Maybe we should be looking for Kurt. God knows he wasn't wrapped too tight. Or how about that creep she prosecuted last year, the one who killed his wife because she was talking to another man, not screwing him, mind you but just talking to the guy about his dog? Didn't he get out on a technical screw up? Or what about that woman who pimped out her two daughters a couple of years ago? I read in the paper that she won her appeal and got out. Didn't she threaten to make Sara disappear."

"So what's your point?"

Amanda pointed to his chin "You missed a spot. My point is that while Borden is definitely not a model citizen, he is not capable of this. He is smart, cunning and doesn't give a rat's ass about anyone besides himself. But he *is* smart and even he wouldn't go to this extreme. Especially since I discredited all of the witnesses."

He put on his undershirt and then the rest of his clothes. He turned to look at her as he tucked in his shirt. "Amanda, let's be real. The guy is accused of killing a child and sadistically carving up the child's mother to get his drug money. Do you really think this guy is going to walk. Doesn't it scare you just a bit that he might be out on the streets tonight?"

She raised an eyebrow, "So, you are conceding that my client might walk"

Walking over to her, he put his arms around her. "No, I'm not conceding anything. What I am saying is that I think you have on rose colored glasses and you are actually buying the shit you are shoveling. Just be careful." He kissed the top of her head and patted her bottom affectionately, "See you at your mom's. I'll be at command central after the closing arguments. I'll call you if we hear anything."

Chapter 12

Sara woke up slowly. She came aware a section at a time. First it was her bladder screaming to be emptied. As she let her mind acknowledge that, she became aware that her mouth felt like it was stuffed with cotton. She ran her hand over her face, trying to push the fog from her brain. Sitting up, she held onto the sit of the cot. It had been reassembled and the mattress was back on it.

As the light blanket slipped from her, she was startled then immediately furious to find that she was completely nude. Mother-fucking-son-of-a-bitch was all that she could think. She stood up then immediately sat back down after the room swam. It took a few more seconds, but she got her bearings and walked over to the port-a-potty. As she sat down she became aware of some muscles that hadn't been used in a while. She reached down and felt the stickiness between her legs. That fucking son of a bitch. He had sex with her. How long was she out? Her foggy brain couldn't quite grasp the passage of time right then. She finished urinating and walked over to the cot and sat down. Looking around she couldn't locate her clothes. Sara got up to get the tray next to the closed door. On a chance she tried the door, only to find that it was still locked. Ass hole had probably put a hasp on the outside. That's what she would have done. And Kurt was no dummy.

As she lifted the tray, she found a stack of pictures underneath it. It was only a few shots, but it showed her having sex with Kurt. She looked out of it, but it was apparent that her ex-husband was enjoying himself. And since his sperm was evident on her, he obviously hadn't practiced safe sex. Good thing I'm on the pill, she thought. Damn, how long had she been here? After a couple of days without the pill, she would surely ovulate. Well, one crisis at a time. As long as he kept drugging her, he was in charge.

She rubbed her arm to warm up and winced. She looked closely at her shoulder and found a small welt. She had been given something through an injection. That would explain how he had kept her down long enough to have sex with her. She snorted, call it what it was. He had raped her. She was going to love letting Pete prosecute this jackass. What the hell was he thinking? That if she got knocked up, she would take him back? That train had left the station six years ago when she finally took a good look at him and realized that he was no better than the losers she was putting behind bars. That was all it took to kill whatever love she had left for him. And now this. There wasn't enough time left on earth to cover the sentence she was going to pursue against him.

Chapter 13

Butler was going over reports from various sources in the states. A terrorist connection had finally been ruled out. As far as the world was concerned, Sara Cohen didn't exist outside of New Jersey. Maybe it was better that way, he thought. Maybe as long as she stayed in the dark about who she was, she'd be safe. And with a powerful and opinionated half brother waiting in the wings, she definitely wasn't safe once she was outed. He put down the papers he had been looking at and looked over at Sara's picture on the crime board. The picture was fairly recent, it showed her in a black power suit giving closing arguments in what had been a particularly gruesome murder case. No, the less the public knew about her, the less the other royals knew about her, the better off she was.

His thoughts were interrupted by Tim coming up and leaning against his desk. "She is quite pretty, isn't she? One thing that has been asked again and again over the years, is why is this Yank a person of interest for the Crown? Her file goes back to the time before she was born. Did the Duke have a fling while out to sea?"

Butler shrugged "I haven't a clue. Like you, I do what I'm told and don't ask too many questions. For all I know, she could be the deposed princess of the Greek isles. There was a whole lot of royals born that year. Maybe she was part of that group. Who knows? All I do know is that she wasn't taken by terrorists. Unless you call the Bloods terrorist?" His lifted eyebrow invited an answer.

Tim shook his head and stood up "They could be called a "home grown" version of terrorist. But they aren't organized enough yet to be a real threat. I agree with you, this isn't some Al-Qaeda plot or any of the ilk. I'm not even seeing the Bloods behind this one. For me, I'm leaning to the ex-hubby as the culprit."

"Me too. So what do we have about this bloke?"

"Kurt Peterson. Born August 1964, in Princeton, New Jersey. Completed secondary, went to college locally and got a degree in business. Worked at an investment firm with some minor success. Married Sara Cohen in 1983. He eventually gambled away his job and his family. They were divorced in 1999 where he dropped off the face of the earth. It was assumed and rumored by informants that he had failed to pay some mafia boss and he got whacked to send a message."

Butler sat back and laced his fingers behind his head. "So, he had a gambling problem but there was no firm proof that he was killed. Let's assume that he isn't dead-that this is his work. Why?"

Tim shrugged "He was probably still in love with her. Couldn't get away from the monkey on his back , so when she cut him loose, he planned to get her back but he had to prove himself."

"Exactly my thinking. Have everything from death records, land purchases, power companies, the whole thing. Any names that come up in common since six years ago. I'd be willing to bet the Queen's garters that he reinvented himself and has a house all set up to take her to and convince her that he's changed."

Chapter 14

Amanda stood and addressed the video camera that would beam her closing arguments to the room where the jury had been sequestered to keep them from view of Borden's supporters. While she had openly denounced what she had called the prosecutions scare tactics, she had been glad that they had been sequestered. Each time a new jury pool had to be vuadered, the more Borden looked guilty.

"Ladies and Gentleman. Thank you for your time. I do realize that this has been an emotional and trying ordeal for all of you. To be separated from your families and jobs. I can only imagine how hard this has been for you, being cooped up in that room for what the prosecution has deemed necessary based on some rumors that you may come to some type of harm while doing your civic duty. Based on a rumor. Just as this case has been based on rumors. The prosecution has presented a case of rumors, not facts.

They haven't provided a shred of existence of an alleged three year old child, nor a body of that child. All they have provided as proof is some blood smear and DNA of a woman, not a child. And even then, the experts could not tell us how old the blood smear was. But a woman, NOT a child. And that is what my client is on trial for. The savage murder of a child. Where is this child? Where is the proof that this child even existed.

And let's not forget the testimony of a drug dealer who also happened to be a convicted thief, who only made the allegation after he was caught robbing a grocery store and needed to cut a deal. Ladies and gentleman, I am not going to insult your intelligence and tell you that the defendant has never bent the law at one point or another. Very few of us can say that. Who amongst us hasn't talked on the cell phone while driving or gone above the speed limit?"

She raised her hand for effect .

"I have. I've received a ticket for doing sixty five in a fifty. But that doesn't make me public enemy number one. Just as it doesn't make any of you a target for the prosecutor.

Unfortunately for my client, because of his associations with various elements in the Trenton area, the prosecutor will go to any lengths, even attempting to convict Mr. Borden based on a rumor. A rumor! Not facts, not bodies strewn about. Rumors. And like all rumors, they may have some grain of truth, like the subject's name. But in this case, that is where it ends. With a name given by a drug dealer in an attempt to cut a deal. Mr. Borden didn't kill a child or torture a woman to get money or revenge. He is innocent of these charges.

You've heard a lot about Mr. Borden's record and previous history, including speeding. But none of those charges have included murder or even assault. My client pays his taxes, supports his family and tries his best to be a law abiding citizen, just like you and me. A conviction based on rumor is nothing but a witch hunt. He is not a monster. He is innocent. Thank you."

Amanda went back to the table and calmly sat down. She would have preferred to see the jury face to face. It was better to make a point when you were able to make eye contact. The emotions came across better. But this wasn't bad. The butterflies in her stomach weren't as bad when you looked at a camera.

Phil got up and went before the camera. He was good. Not as good as Sara, a bit stiff and mechanical, but his voice carried conviction and sometimes that was all it took.

"I too want to thank you for your time. Those county hotels aren't the best. Those mattresses need to be flipped once in a while, I know, having stayed in them a time or two myself." He paused for what he knew was a chuckle

I'd like all of you to look at Mr. Borden and look hard. Ms. Inverso says that Mr. Borden is a tax paying citizen just like the rest of us. That our whole case is based on rumor.

And I tell you that it's not based on rumor, but the eye witness testimony of a grieving father who had to watch while this monster killed his child and tortured the child's mother over drugs and money. The very same mother who was gunned down on the steps of this very court house by those elements that Mr. Borden associates with.

There may not have been documented proof that this child existed with the exception of his father telling you that he existed. Malcolm Rayshawn Sutton. He was born at home, loved by his parents and killed by the monster before you. It is that monster who should be put behind bars. If a tree falls in the woods and no one is there to hear it, does it still make a noise? Just because little Malcolm didn't have a birth certificate doesn't mean that he didn't make a noise. We need to get Mr. Borden off the streets and behind bars so that he cannot hurt and kill anyone else. Thank you, ladies and gentlemen."

Amanda schooled her face not to reflect an emotion but inside she was sweating. Nothing like intelligence and conviction to sway a jury. No matter how much you shredded the experts, presented proof and cast doubt, a good closing argument could sway a jury one way or another.

The judge was talking to the camera giving the jury instructions on the charges and what they were deliberating about. Then he banged the gavel and recessed the court while the jury deliberated. Amanda and Borden stood to leave the room. As they walked to the outer area and toward the conference rooms, a sheriff was trailing them. Hakiem looked over at the deputy and waved. He held the door for Amanda then entered it himself. Closing the door behind them he went to the table and pulled out the chair for her. He sat down and straightened his tie. "I owe you an apology for yesterday. You caught me out there, I didn't expect you to talk about losing."

She shook her head. "I understand, Hakiem. I just wanted you to be prepared for anything. We need to stay in here until the jury comes back or the judge recesses for the night. How about we order some lunch? Fabulous' delivers and they make a great cheeses steak."

Hakiem chuckled, "Lady, who you talking to? Fabulous and I go way back. We can even get it for free." He pulled his cell phone out of his suit jacket.

Amanda gave him an appraising look. She had told him to get two suits, charcoal gray and dark blue, no pin stripes or anything flashy. Low key and humble was what she was going for. Even his ties were low key and humble, everything signaling that he was just a simple man caught up in circumstance beyond his control.

The young man was definitely charismatic and exuded power. With his bone structure and mocha coloring, Hakiem could have graced the cover of GQ or Esquire. If he had been directed in the right direction, he could have been someone. There was no doubt that he was very intelligent and when he wanted to, he had excellent speaking skills, leaving the hood Ebonics at the door.

But, it was a good thing that the jury hadn't seen him outside of the court room. With his "ghetto hood" inspired velour sweat suit and ball cap twisted to one side, his swagger and attitude left know doubt in Amanda's mind that he was capable of what he was being accused of.

She had almost turned him away until she saw a picture of two kids on his key ring. The picture turned out to be of his niece and nephew. Their mother had died in a drug o.d. and he had been raising them with his girlfriend.

When he talked about them, Amanda saw his face soften and in that moment, she knew that he wouldn't have killed a child. Hakiem had admitted to her that he had beaten the murdered woman so badly that she had to go to the hospital for a few days, but that the dealer had given him his money. He drew the line at hurting kids. Amanda believed him. She could live with adults bringing their own hell down on themselves, but anything done to a child was intolerable. It also didn't hurt that he could meet her ten grand walk in the door fee, fifteen hundred an hour plus expenses. It didn't hurt that her success rate was ninety eight percent. She had lost two cases in eight years. Not too shabby. And in one of those cases she had won on appeal.

"I'll take onions and mushrooms on mine" she told him.

Chapter 15

Tim looked at the computer screen and tapped a few more keys. It felt like it was going to be forever wading through this much information. By the time the cross referencing between all of the points came together, there were more than eleven hundred people to check out. He ran another eliminator through the data. He was looking for a single male. It stood to reason that if Peterson was setting up a household under an assumed name it would be better and require less explanations if he listed as a single male.

Still left eight hundred and sixteen. He ran the obit filter on it and the list dropped down to three hundred and twenty three. That many people still using the dead people's info? Nothing like fraud to keep a person in the life style that they had become accustomed to.

He had included the immediate Pennsylvania area as well. Philadelphia alone accounted for 180 of the 323.

If they stuck with the presumption that the ex had taken her, it had to be that he was holding her to either convince her to come back or to torture her. Either way, he was going to need privacy. So that ruled out apartment buildings or multi family dwellings. That dropped the list down to less than 200. Since the bridges and roadways into New York hadn't revealed the van crossing there, it took New York out of the running. Tim mentally shuddered at the thought. If the van had made it into the City, the the odds against finding her became astronomical.

He ran a program on the list looking for floor plans with basements. It was a hope of his that they would get lucky. Butler looked over the flat screen monitor and smiled. "Please tell me that you've got something."

Shaking his head and leaning back Tim took a deep breath. "Sorry, chap. This list is unbelievable. Based on names, dates and other factors, I've narrowed it down to under 200, but not by much. Remember that this guy has had six years to plan this. Unless we catch a break someplace, she's gone until he's ready to let her go."

Butler stood beside Tim's desk to look at the monitor. One of the computer techs slid over a chair for him then left the room. Taking a seat in the vacated chair, Butler motioned for the keyboard.

He slid it over and turned the screen for better viewing. "I had the eggheads at the Yard run the numbers and probabilities for escape routes. Then I talked to the doctors about various medications and what not. So, Peterson sprays her with mace, then tasers her and throws her into the van. He drives off with her immobilized, but that doesn't last long. So he has to drug her. And it has to be by injection or inhalation. She isn't willingly going to take a pill or a drink..."

"Unless he tricks her by spiking her water or food."

"Yeah, I thought of that too. But let's give our girl some credit for sense here. "

"Butler, I've been thinking about something. That van, the plates were bogus and everyone assumed that she was taken by the van because the cameras showed a van pulling in behind her and leaving after she did."

"Yeah, so what's your point?"

"The parking garage, it's unmanned. What if Peterson didn't drive the van. What if he had a car in the parking garage and pulled her out of the car and loaded it into a car that he had waiting? He could have maced her, shocked her, opened the car and had her out in under a minute. It would have looked like he was helping her if someone really looked."

Butler leaned back in his chair and let it roll around in his brain for a second. "Why didn't the driver of the van stop?"

Tim raised an eyebrow "Are you serious? How long have you been out of the States? A man arguing with a woman would look like a domestic. And since the van was probably stolen, the last thing one of these bloke's wants is to get involved. He would have gotten out of there as fast as possible."

"I'll be damned. I went on the same assumptions as the locals. You're right. Let's pull the tapes again as well as the other exits and camera films from the traffic lights. I feel another sleepless night coming, but I have an even bigger feeling that you're on the right track."

Chapter 16

_____

The tray was shoved through the slot in the door. He must have a camera looking at her somewhere. How else would he know she was awake? Her first impulse was to throw the food against the door. Then she thought better. He was trying to break her.

Drugs, sex and kidnapping. It was almost text book. Almost. Since she had read that book, she knew that the sooner she looked like she was sympathetic to his cause the sooner she would be able to find an escape route. She looked at the food tray again. She couldn't appear to break to soon. But she sure as hell didn't fell like having unconscious sex again.

She took the water from the tray and opened it and pretended to drink from it. She sat on the bed and waited. Nothing. O.K. it wasn't the water. So it had to be the food. She picked up the salad and the tuna fish sandwich. She took a bite of the sandwich and pretended to mull it over. The bitter aftertaste in the mayo was the clue. She took a small sip of the water, put it down on the tray and lay back down on the bed.

She tried her best to look sleepy, which wasn't too hard because whatever he had slipped into her sandwich was pretty strong. She stretched out on the bed and covered herself with the blanket. Before too long she let out a light snore. If he was watching he was also probably listening. Might as well give a good performance.

The light in the room began to dim and the door slowly opened. There was probably a dimmer switch outside the door, she thought. Something to keep in the back of her mind. She wasn't sure how it would help, but every bit of information was valuable.

Kurt walked up to the cot and knelt down beside it. He rubbed a cautious hand over her hair. It took everything in her not to flinch or stiffen. He continued to stroke her hair back from her face. Sara was surprised when he let out a small sob and burrowed his head into her shoulder.

"I love you so much, Sara. I really screwed up. I forgot to put you and the girls first and it cost me everything. But when you wake up, I'll show you how I've turned everything around. I have a house now. A good job and I joined gambler's anonymous. I haven't placed a bet or even went into a casino in five years. I still love you and if you give me a chance, I'll prove it to you. I swear. I've changed. You'll see." He bent over her and kissed her lips. He stayed that way for a few seconds. Then wiping the tears from his face, he stood and walked out of the room.

Sara heard the lock slide into the door jamb. She was too shocked and surprised to move. Instead she lay there, thinking about what he said. Five years not gambling. There had to be something to that. She let sleep overcome her, the last thought going through her mind was at least he didn't try to feel her up.

Chapter 17

Butler came awake instantly. It was something he had been able to do since infancy. His mother had often remarked how he was like a dolphin, never completely asleep, always on his feet at the first sign of something interesting. This time it was the tapping of a pigeon on his room window. It was barely first light. He looked at his watch. He had been asleep for three hours. Well, if he could hear the pigeons, his brain must have gotten all of the rest that it needed. He hit the shower, shaved, brushed his teeth and was on his way down the stairs to command central in ten minutes. There was no sign of Tim, but his computer was chugging away at something. The coffee pot was half empty and a steaming mug was on Tim's desk. He must have stepped out for a cigarette. Butler sat at the desk across from Tim's and logged in. He opened the secure e-mail from London. MI-6 agreed that it wasn't a terrorist plot and it was local. No shit, he thought.

The sound of buttons being pushed on the lock to the door announced Tim's return. He sat and picked up his mug, taking a big gulp out of it. He reeked of smoke. Butler never smoked and couldn't get over how others could in this day and age. Well, to each his own.

"I've been running all the names in the systems and finding some interesting matches. I've restricted it to just New Jersey and New York and the surrounding area of Pennsylvania. We've come up with six possibilities. One of the interesting ones that we are going to drive out to today is a match with a match with a match."

Butler raised an eyebrow "how's that?"

"Well, I found a match between one of the plates from the garage and a power bill then a cable bill to a house address but the house is registered to another name from a credit card. With this many strings all leading in different directions, I get a little tingle in my nads and have to follow it."

"A tingle, huh? How big of a tingle?"

"Big enough that if we were playing at home, I'd be taking some toys and boys with us."

"And you're hesitating why?"

That made him put his cup down. "Because...we are in someone else's jurisdiction and that tends to piss the locals off. And we don't have enough to go on other than a bunch of dots that connect everywhere but nothing concrete not too mention that I could be wrong."

Butler shook his head. "I looked at everything that you have here and I agree. As far as the locals, this is a British intelligence operation. And as far as the locals are concerned, we have a missing British National, so all bets are off. "

"Since when has an American Jew become a British National, there mate?"

"Since I decided that she was one. Get the Team ready, we leave in fifteen minutes. I'll call home and tell them to prepare something when this hits the wall." He picked up the phone to make a secured line call, leaving Tim with his thoughts and lots of questions.

Chapter 18

Amanda was back at the defendant's table in the court room. The jury had been out for the rest of the day before and had reconvened that morning. It was now nearly lunch and word was sent that a verdict still had not been reached.

Amanda knew that she had done her job right. There had been no evidence that the child had even been born. No hospital records, no prenatal care, no welfare payments. Even the pictures of the house where the alleged baby had lived had no crib, no clothes not even diapers or baby toys to show that a child had ever been there.

The witness had testified that the death of the baby had been so terrible to him and his girlfriend, that they had gotten rid of all evidence that he had been there.

Doctor's reports had been inconclusive as to when the supposed mother had given birth.

She had five children in rapid succession and was pregnant at the time of her murder. The medical examiner had testified that due to her drug use, her many pregnancies and miscarriages, it was difficult to correctly determine if she had given birth in between her last living child and the pregnancy at the time of her death.

Her other children, all born in hospitals, had been in the care of the state since she was a heavy drug user and couldn't care for them. Amanda had nearly jumped for joy when that evidence had come to light. The drug dealer told the court that they had kept the baby's birth a secret because the state would have taken him away.

All in all, there was no proof that the child existed.

The video camera came on and the twenty people in the jury room somewhere in the building filed into the room. The bailiff stepped forward and took a folded piece of paper from a man amongst the twenty individuals.

The judge looked at the camera just as if he were speaking to them there in the court room. "Ladies and Gentleman. It is my understanding that you have a request?

One of the jurors (since it had been agreed that there would be a different foreperson everyday) stood and addressed the camera in their room "Your honor. We would like to speak with the DYFS worker handling the children from the dead woman. We would also like the coroner's report of the dead woman.

"Is that all for now?"

"Yes your Honor."

"Fine. The items will be delivered to you shortly."

The T.V. monitor went black and the judge faced Amanda and Hakiem.

"Counselors, it looks like we will be waiting for some more time. I will have my clerk call you when they have a decision. Since I will be recessing for the day in an hour, let's call it a day." The judge banged the gavel and left the bench. Amanda and Hakiem left the room and went back to the lawyers room where Amanda did a little happy dance as soon as the door was closed. Hakiem looked at her with puzzled humor.

"You are acting like we won."

"Forgive me. I beg your pardon, but did you hear the jury? They referred to her as the woman, not the baby's momma.

That is an indication that they are not convinced that there was a baby."

"I didn't catch that. But thinking about it, you are probably right. So we're done for the day?"

"I'll call you if we hear anything tonight. If not, I will see you here tomorrow at eight."

They turned toward the door and started to leave.

"Thank you Miss Inverso. Thank you for working so hard for me. You are worth every dime we had to spend."

She patted his back as she walked with him. "I'm glad you feel that way. Now let's hope my sister comes home in one piece."

Hakiem suddenly looked angry. "Excuse me, but if you'se suggestin' that I had summtin to do wit dat, that's some bullshit"

"Mr. Borden, I didn't mean to suggest that you had anything to do with her disappearance. But if you hear something or run across someone who may have seen something, it would help."

He rolled his lips together so that they disappeared into his mouth. He slowly nodded. "Tell you what, Miss Inverso. Lemme see whats I can finze out. Maybe your peeps ain't lookin' where we do, feel me?" gone was the sleek educated young man and back was the street thug. He swaggered out of the court room followed by a half dozen other young men. Amanda shook her head. She was sure that while this was the first time that she had done business with Hakiem Borden, it wouldn't be the last for him or his posse. As she shifted her briefcase and opened the door, her phone vibrated in her pocket.

Chapter 20

Dressed in black and wearing riot gear, all of the team had on flack vests with the word "Police" in big yellow letters emblazoned on the back. Anyone looking out of the windows would assume that it was a local police operation. A rapid check around the house indicated that it was a one level with a basement. All of the basement windows were painted black and locked. They were barely big enough for a small child to get through so that wasn't an option, but it was the most likely place that Sara was being held. A visual confirmation of Kurt was made. He was sitting in the dining room with a cup of coffee looking at a tele news broadcast of the continuing man-hunt and search for Sara Cohen and anyone having information regarding her disappearance was encouraged to call the police.

Butler signaled for two of the Team to go to the left and two to the right. They would be going through the side windows. Tim would be going through the front with a member and Butler would take the back with the last member of the Team. That would be all of them. Hopefully that would be all that they needed. Through the mic attached to his throat, Butler gave the order and as one they crashed into the house. Kurt was so surprised and shocked that he was momentarily stunned.

Before he could grab the stun gun that was on the table next to him, Butler had him by the throat and was shoving him onto the floor. A series of "clear" went through the ear piece as Butler cuffed Kurt and roughly flipped him over. Adopting an American accent had been decided at the beginning of the mission. The fewer things that stuck out, the less questions that had to be answered. "Where is Sara Cohen?"

Kurt sputtered "I don't know a Sara Cohen. Who the hell are you?"

"Really Kurt. We know you were in the parking garage when she was snatched and since she's your *ex-wife*, I would assume you know who she is. NOW TELL ME WHERE THE FUCK SHE IS OR I'LL SMASH YOUR HEAD RIGHT INTO THE FLOOR!" He gave Kurt's head a small bounce into the floor for effect.

"All right, all right! She's in the basement. The key is hanging on the door frame."

Butler flipped him over and cuffed him. After Kurt was secured, Butler got off of him and motioned for one of the Team to watch him. It was understood that the less that was said, the easier things would be to explain.

Another Team member came into the room "Sir, I think you should see this." The young woman used a southern drawl to disguise her British accent.

Butler and Tim followed her to another room off of the kitchen. The room was a virtual shrine to Sara. As well as the half dozen monitors that showed the room that Sara was in from every conceivable angle. Butler uttered a curse under his breath when he noticed the pictures of an unconscious Sara having sex with Kurt. His blood boiled and he turned on his heel. From the murderous expression on his face, Tim knew the guy was going to get the beating of his life. He reached out and grabbed his friend's arm.

"Butler, wait. I know what you want to do. But stop and think. This is going to be hot enough and if you do anything else, the bugger's going to get off. I think I have a good plan to reduce our explaining."

That stopped him. "Well?"

"We leave everything the way it is, including jackass on the floor, cuffed. Have Riggins here phone in an anonymous tip about seeing some unsavory characters breaking in. The locals come in, discover our friend on the floor and save Sara. We are left with the mission completed and very little to explain or cover up."

As much as Butler wanted to get physical with Kurt, he knew that Tim was right. Better to not have to explain anything than to have to come up with a good cover story.

They reassembled in the kitchen and filed out, making sure that they weren't observed by any of the neighbors.

Tim and Butler were the last to leave. Kurt was looking around and squirming about, trying to get a better look at them as they left. "Hey, what's going on? You can't leave me like this. What kind of cops are you? I want my lawyer, I don't know who you are, but you can't do this to me." His voice was growing increasingly strident.

Tim and Butler looked at each other. Butler took a step to Kurt and with one swing punched him in the jaw. It was hard enough to knock him out cold. He gave a small smile of satisfaction and looked at his partner.

Tim shrugged, "Well, some realism is called for." They left the door open and signaled for Riggins to make the call. They were rounding the corner as a squad car same speeding past them. As the Team drove down the street, the were passed by several more squad cars, lights and sirens cutting a path through the mid-day traffic. As the truck went over the bridge and back into the city, they listened to the police band as Sara was discovered and rescued. The last report was her going to the hospital and the Mercer County Prosecutor's Office being called. And a happy ending was had by all, Butler thought. But he couldn't shake the feeling that this wasn't the end of things.

Chapter 21

Sara was getting dressed in the clothes her mother had brought for her. The clothes that she had been abducted in were being held as evidence. Not that they were really going to be needed. It was a slam dunk as far as she was concerned. The pictures, the DNA samples that the CSU had gathered. Kurt had even video taped everything from start to finish. One way or another he was going to spend the rest of his life in a cage.

Someone clearing his throat from the other side of the curtain made her straighten up. She finished buttoning her jeans and slipped on her sweatshirt. Leave it to her mom to know how to make her feel safe. "Come in."

Pete peaked around the curtain. "I was going to make some kind of ass hole joke, but I figured you could use a break for the moment, all things considered."

Sara gave a snort and sat on the bed to put on her sneakers. "Thanks. It took you guys long enough to rescue me. How'd you figure out where I was?"

Her boss shook his head and leaned against the wall. "That's the thing, we didn't. Some guys broke into Kurt's house and saw all the video equipment, you being held hostage and called in the tip. Go figure. Crooks with a conscious. We weren't even looking in that direction. We were still working the Bloods angle."

"Really? I already heard, by the way. Ma said she didn't know if she should strangle Amanda or cheer for her. And she was right, you know. We would have done the same thing, both of us. I can't really blame her. Doesn't mean that I'm not going to give her shit about it when I get out of here. What time is Kurt's arraignment?"

Pete shifted his feet and looked uncomfortable "Yeah, about that. He's currently being held at the Camden lock-up in the psyche ward. His attorney is screaming police brutality and he has a broken jaw to substantiate the call. Not too mention that there is a shit load of evidence to support an insanity plea…."

Her other shoe dropped to the floor as the strength left her arms in disbelief. "No, don't say it. Come on. You can't be fucking serious. He's copping a diminished capacity plea. Are you kidding me? After all of this, he's going to go to a mental hospital? Whose fucking bright idea was that?!"

"Not mine, that's for sure. This was moved out of Mercer County because of jurisdiction of the bust, not where the crime was originally committed. And since a ransom was never made and there were no organized crime ties, the Feds have no pull here. Camden is making this out to be a psyche and not a domestic."

"Well, at least he will be off the streets for no less than five years. That's a guarantee. State law mandates that sentence. Camden P.D. is trying to keep this out of the papers as much as possible. Even though they weren't the ones to break Kurt's face, it doesn't look good for them."

"So, the son of a bitch is going to get away with a slap on the wrist. He kidnapped me, raped me, held me captive in a dungeon, drugged me and he is going to stay in a nice cushy mental hospital for five years instead of Trenton state where he can be someone's cell block bitch for the next eighteen years? Where the hell is the justice in that?"

Pete looked down at the floor and shook his head again. He looked up at her face, tears of rage brimming in her eyes "I'm sorry to be the one to tell you this, honey, but sometimes there is no justice. Sometimes the bad guys get the breaks and we just have to live with it. I know it sucks, but there isn't much we can do about it."

She bent over and picked up her sneaker. Wiping away a tear, she slipped the shoe on and tied it. Standing up she took a deep breath. "Well, it sucks."

Her friend stood and faced her, placing his hands on her shoulders and pressed his forehead to hers. Looking her in the eye he felt her pain "I know, Honey. It sucks like hell. How about we go see my nieces and my wife then get shit faced drunk at your house? I know a couple of attorneys who have been through hell lately that could use a whole lot of stress relief."

Chapter 23

He was putting the last of his gear in his carry sack, preparing to catch his flight. Butler had done this countless times without a single thought about where he was going next. Only this time, something was different. A feeling of dread overwhelmed him and made him sit down. He had no home to go to. Sure he had his flat in Nottingham. But it was empty. Kate had made it a home, she had brought warmth and light to it, to him and now it was gone.

With everything in his heart, he didn't want to go back and face what he knew he had to do. He knew that he had to pack up her things, clean out and give away what was no longer going to be used. All the things that widowers did to help them move on. Things that he had been avoiding for the past few months. But he just couldn't. If he packed away her things, it would be like burying her again. It would be signal to his heart that she was never coming back. He wasn't sure that he could survive it.

He rubbed a hand over his face and tried to center himself inside. He checked his watch. The flight was scheduled to leave in two hours. This time tomorrow, he would be in his flat, staring at the wall and reliving Kate. The vibration from the phone on his belt broke into his grief. Truth be told, he wasn't sure if he was relieved or annoyed.

He looked at the number and flipped it open "yeah Chief"

"Unpack, you're not coming home just yet. Our computer people just informed me that someone managed to get into the medical records of the royals."

"I thought that was impossible, or at least highly unlikely."

"Yeah, they thought so too. Medical records aren't as tightly held as other things. The reason that I'm keeping you there is that while they couldn't trace who broke in, the geeks tell me that a ghost of the images was intercepted and it was the DNA profile of the royals and the first line ascension."

"So, someone has suspicions about the princess."

"Butler, we can't be sure. Laraby thinks it's a fishing expedition, but I want to make sure. Someone has managed to put two and two together, I need to know if they came up with the right answer."

"What about the Intel chatter?"

"That's another thing. It's too quite. And while frankly, I like it when things die down, on the heels of our kidnapping, I feel like something big is coming down the pipe and I don't want to step in it. Find something, anything and stay close to the princess. Out"

The connection was broken by James. He was a man of few words, never mind the niceties. Butler was used to it. The last time that James had closed with a "goodbye" was the day after Kate had died. James had called to tell him that he was on bereavement leave. No "sorry for your loss" or "take as much time as you need". No- just "you are on bereavement leave and click. Nice to know that some things never change.

Butler looked at the closed phone for a second then hooked it back onto his belt. Well, if he was going to watch the princess, he had better get a place on the other side of the water. He picked up his bag and walked out, a little relieved. He wouldn't be returning to his empty flat too soon.

Chapter 24

Tim looked up from the computer monitor to watch Butler come into the parlor. Good man, he thought. A little dour, but what with Kate dying and all, who would blame him. "Ready to go home?"

Butler shook his head "Nope. Looks like I'm staying a little while longer. Bancroft said that someone hacked into the system and got a peak at something that made him nervous. I'm assigned to here for a time, until the computer people get to the bottom of it."

Sitting back from the desk a little, Tim leaned back and balanced on the chairs rear legs. "Really. What kind of info?"

"I'm not at liberty to say, but I have to ask you. How many of your team here are computer smart?"

Lifting a brow in surprise "All of them. It was one of the prerequisites to be assigned here. Why do you ask?"

"The information was hard to get. Mind you, not impossible and not something that anyone thought as damaging or dangerous, but it wasn't easy to erase their steps. That takes some skill. I know you trust them, but we need to take a hard look at everyone on your team. I don't want to get caught with my knickers down about my ankles."

Letting the chair fall forward, Tim started typing into the computer's keyboard. "While a part of me is highly insulted, Butler old boy, I've seen enough of those movies to know that there has to be some truth to what you're saying. So let's begin with the most senior and work our way down, shall we?"

Chapter 25

Sara stood under the spray of the shower in her bathroom. She wasn't spooked enough to leave the door open, but the garbage can was in front of the door in case someone tried to get in. She knew she was being overly cautious, but she wasn't going to let it happen again.

She went through her normal Saturday routine. The girls had soccer games this morning. And while all she wanted to do was get behind the computer and help put Kurt away forever, she wasn't going to hurt the girls any more by further disrupting their lives. The weekends were sacred to Sara.

She spent so many hours at work that this was the only time that she had to make sure that she connected with Cassidy and T.J.. This was something she never compromised on. It helped that her family was so close together. They all pitched in when needed.

She turned off the shower and stepped onto the bath rug. It needed to be replaced. It was one of those things that she always told herself, but was promptly forgotten in the course of a very busy day.

Checking the clock on the wall she went into overdrive. Quick moisturizer, a little mascara and some lip stick, she was off and running. As she flew into her clothes, she listened with a mother's ear to the girls fighting in the kitchen about socks. It was a never ending battle. Cassidy was highly organized and never misplaced anything. T.J. on the other hand would spend an hour looking for a pair of soccer socks, even though each girl had at least three pairs.

Running down the stairs, Sara stopped at the sock basket near the door heading into the laundry room. She rummaged around for a few seconds, came up with a pair and sailed into the kitchen. She hung them on T.J.'s shoulder. "I told you a hundred times, either look in the drawer or look in the basket. T.J., you're old enough to start keeping track of your own stuff. This is getting really old.

Did you guys eat? Where's the water bottles? Where are your bags? Come on! Chop Chop! We gotta go." Same drill done over and over again. But there was a strange comfort in it. Something normal. As they walked out of the door and to the car, Sara couldn't help feeling that she was being watched. It was so strong that she looked around. No strange cars or people walking along. She checked the door behind her and got into the car. The thought of a guard dog ran through her mind, very briefly. As she backed the car out of the driveway, she looked around again. Locking the cars doors, she felt a little better, but only a little.

Chapter 26

As Butler closed another file on the computer a thought occurred to him. Why the hell was he wasting time trying to figure out who the inside person was. By the time he figured it out, it might be too late. It was obvious that someone was sniffing around and it wouldn't be long before the truth was out. He got up from his chair. Not one to wait for the snake to strike, he grabbed his bag and without a word to Tim, he went out the door.

He pulled out his phone and dialed a series of numbers. It was to James' cell phone, his private one that only three people in the world knew.

"James, I had a thought and I'm going with it. I'm going to go into deep cover for awhile."

"Really?" James sounded a little surprised. It wasn't in Butler's nature to go subtle, undercover. Butler had been mildly reprimanded in the past for his brash nature.

"We're searching for a mole and I'm along with you that it won't be long before the secret is out. That being the case, I'm going to do what the Yanks call a pre-emptive strike. I'll be traveling way off the radar."

"Well, just watch yourself down there. I don't need to remind you that if things prove necessary, the secret may have to be taken out of the equation."

Butler stopped in his tracks. That got his attention. "Are you telling me that I need to make the secret disappear? That would make things a hell of a lot easier, if you ask me."

"Not yet. I've presented it to the founder of this secret and while they are ademently against it, the lady has the final word. Should it prove necessary, it might be a requirement. We're going to keep it on the back-burner as it were, for now anyhow."

"Hell of a back burner, if you ask me."

"Butler, if you run into something that I should know about, call me. Don"t let me hear it on the internet, thank you."

"Got it."

He closed his phone and slipped it back onto his belt. This made things interesting. He stopped by a diner that advertised wi-fi. Time to set things into motion.

Chapter 27

Another Monday morning, she thought. Sara's rented mini-van pulled up in front of the girls' school in line with the other string of mini-vans that were the commonality of this neighborhood. All of the kids arrived at the same time, so the queue stretched far down the street as other parents waited to begin the day. Pulling up to the curb, she pushed a button that let her daughters out to what Cassidy called the "Child storage facility".

It was convenient that the elementary school, the middle school and the high school were all on the same block. It made for a huge compound with all the schools sharing a common athletic field and track, but the parents loved the convenience.

She wanted to be homed schooled. Sara wished she could do it, but neither of them would last too long if they went that route. Cassidy was just as head strong as her mother and even at fifteen years old, they often got into battles of the will.

After quick pecks and even faster hugs, the girls were out and the door closed with the push of a button. Sara liked the bells and whistles. When it came time to get a new van, this might be the one she settled on.

She signaled and pulled away from the curb. As she melted into the traffic, her brain began to shift gears and got into the work mode.

The jury was still out. Since they had not come to a verdict on Friday, the judge let them have the weekend off to think as individuals.

They had all known that it had been a long shot when they brought it to the grand jury. It was the testimony of a grieving father that had convinced the grand jury to bring about charges. But the Prosecutor's Office had been grasping at straws when they had presented the case. They were desperate to get Borden off the streets and behind bars. It wouldn't totally nullify his authority on the streets, but it might slow some of the activity down. In Trenton and some of the surrounding townships, that was they best that they could hope for. And every day, the war zone that was the capital of New Jersey got wider and wider.

Bastions of untouchable neighborhoods were getting sucked in faster and faster. Some of the Mafia strongholds were falling to the Bloods and the Crips because of the government's targeting of the mob. By taking away the mafia muscle, it was leaving the neighborhoods defenseless against the up and coming gangs.

As much as the Feds hated to admit it, the mob served a purpose. And until the Feds took the Bloods and the Crips seriously, it wasn't going to get any better. Sara reflected that the government had been the same way when it came to the KKK and the Black Panthers. Until blood was spilled on T.V., it didn't exist.

She pulled into the lot and showed her I.D. to the now present guard in a booth. As Sara drove to her assigned spot, she saw county workers installing cameras. At least something positive came of all this, she thought. Now there wasn't a space of the garage or the surrounding area that wasn't covered. A sheriff's deputy would now be posted 24/7 at the monitor to set off an alarm should anything else happen. Sure, she thought, now after my world was turned upside down.

Which brought her around to Kurt's arraignment that was scheduled for nine that morning. Since his arrest occurred in Camden county, the Camden Prosecutor was going to be handling it. Especially since the crime was committed against a Mercer County D.A.. Phil and Paul were going to the courthouse up there so she wouldn't have to. She had spent the weekend going through possible defenses. It was going to be a real pain, but she was going to have to testify and recount everything that she could remember. She and Amanda had played out every possible scenario that he could use as a defense. She had sided with her sister against her boss/brother-in-law. Sara completely agreed that her sister did the right thing in continuing with the case. Giving a mental shrug, she would have done the same thing in her position.

She opened the van's side door and got out her brief case and umbrella. It looked like rain and she hated doing the mad dash from the parking garage to the building in pouring rain. She walked passed the guard in his little shack. He gave her a little wave and checked her name off on a clip board. They were now checking to see who came and went. Another change.

Glancing up at the cloudy sky, she gave a small shake as a shiver ran up her spine. Her grandmother had a touch of the gift, sort of a sixth sense. It reminded Sara of her, the clouds gathering and a sense of foreboding. Something was definitely heading her way, and it wasn't good.

Chapter 28

Butler pulled into the lot right behind Sara. He showed his credentials to the guard in the little shack. A nice, older gentleman. Obviously a retired cop, he compared Butler's picture and passport with his face. Butler's credentials identified him as a legal attaché to the British Consulate. Butler also handed over a letter of introduction from the Consulate stating that he was part of the advance team holding interviews for a new trade agreement between Great Britain and the U.S.

If anyone called the number, the call would be directed to the M.I.-6 office in London and his story would be confirmed. He had already set the cover up as a fall-back, instant cover. The cover was maintained by the consulate in case an emergency came up and instant insertion was needed. All countries did it. That was one of the reasons no one was totally sure who was a player and who was legitimate.

He parked in the space that he had been assigned marked "visitor". He retrieved his briefcase from the car and locked it up. In the case were documents pertaining to a trade agreement that was currently being discussed between the U.S. and G.B. that much had been true. All good lies are ninety-eight percent truth. It was that two percent that made all the difference. He crossed over to the modern courthouse building and went through the doors. He was directed by the sheriff's deputy to put his brief case on the conveyor belt and went through the metal detector. When the x-ray machine was unable to penetrate the brief case, Butler held up his i.d. to the sheriff.

"I apologize Sheriff. I'm a legal attaché with the British Consulate in New York. You're welcomed to go through the case, but our brief cases are always lined."

The sheriff deputy looked annoyed, but nodded. Butler moved over to the case and dialed in the code to open the largest area of the briefcase. The deputy ruffled the files and patted the folders to make sure that there were no guns, knives or anything else that could make life interesting. After he was satisfied that Butler wasn't a threat, he told him "thanks" and pointed him to the other deputy that was waiting to pat him down. For some reason, she was taking her time to pat him down. And unlike the male deputy, she had no problem getting between his legs. What made Butler grin was that she never cracked a smile.

He looked her in the eyes and smiled "Thank you officer. I haven't had that much fun since last weekend."

Without missing a beat, never cracking a smile "I'm sorry to hear that sir, but you'd be surprised what can be hidden between a man's legs. Have a good day sir."

What they didn't know was hidden inside a very thin pocket was a wireless transmitter, a multi-tool, a small .22 caliber gun and a taser. Things that a good agent never left home without.

Going over to the large wooden counter/desk area, Butler asked for directions to Sara's office. He already knew where it was, having gone over the floor plans, but to maintain his cover, he had to make it look good. He took the elevator to the third floor and exited to the left. Walking down the hallway he made out whose name was on the doors and who was talking with whom. He passed people lining the hallway sitting on the benches. Some were obviously nervous, some were relaxed but they all had one thing in common. They were all part of the great American legal system.

He made his way down the hall until he came to a door marked "Asst. D.A." Very unremarkable, considering how many lives were changed by what happened behind the door. He opened it and found himself in a small waiting area that led to three other doors. Each door was labeled to a different lawyer. He knocked on Sara's and was told to "come in". As he slowly opened the door, the smell of fresh brewed coffee welcomed him in. He smiled, it was hazelnut. A flavor he had grown to like every time he came to the States. The flavor and scents weren't that big back home. Nice to see the lady had good taste.

She looked up at him over her half glasses and assessed him. God, he's hot ran through her mind. Her second thought was that he wasn't local. "Can I help you?"

He approached her and stretched out his hand "Hello. My name is Harold Marshall. You went to University with my sister, Catherine."

Sara stood up and took his hand in a warm shake. "Well, I'll be damned. Catherine told me so much about you. Please, have a seat. Would you like some coffee?"

"If it wouldn't be too much of a bother. I hate to say it, but I have gotten extremely fond of your American coffee. We don't get such stuff on my side of the pond. It's one of the things that I have FedExed back to my flat whenever I come over. Being a legal attaché has to have some perks."

Sara handed him the Styrofoam cup. "Is black all right?"

He inhaled the steam deeply "I wouldn't have it any other way"

She returned to her chair and pulled herself in. "How is Catherine? I've been meaning to e-mail her, but things are busier than you could imagine."

Butler nodded. "I read about what happened to you and so did Catherine. I promised her that the second I could break away, that I would come over and personally check on you."

"Yeah, well it has been a memorable week. But, I'm working through it. So what brings you to the States?"

"I'm working for the consulate right now. We're putting together the trade agreement between G.B. and that U.S. for military equipment and personnel. Sort of, you give us some of yours and we'll give you some of ours. My job is to go through the proposed personnel and make sure that they are squeaky clean."

Sara gave a small laugh "What, you hoisted the less than stellar British off on us, you want to make sure we don't return the favor?"

"Something like that. Seriously, with all of this Al-Qaeda crap, we have to make sure that the only ones going over are at least third generation or better."

"You're serious?"

"Definitely. I told my boss that maybe we should just go to one of your reservations and draft the personnel from there. At least we'd know for sure where they came from."

"As a local lawyer, I wouldn't advise that. The government is hell bent on proving that most of the Natives aren't Natives and the Natives are holding on with both hands to their lands and trying to prove that their people were here first."

"Really? I thought that the Natives were happy living on the third world styled reservations or building up casinos. So, the Natives are getting restless?"

With a groan, Sara gave her head a slight smack on the desk. "Catherine always told me that you have a warped sense of humor. She didn't tell me how warped. So, what is Cat up to these days?"

"She got her wig, got into a nice practice and is up for partner."

"Is she still doing Civil Rights?"

"Of course. She got bit by the activist bug over here and took it home. Mostly stuff out of South Africa and believe it or not, here in the States. Seems some of our lads got tangled up in some nasty little stuff and sent to Gitmo."

"I've heard about that place. If I were a betting woman, I'd wager that place isn't going to be open for too much longer. I heard Amnesty International was getting involved."

Butler looked at his watch. "Sara, I do hate to suck down your coffee and run, but I'm due at a background check here in the Trenton area in about an hour and that GPS isn't able to tell me the good neighborhoods from the bad."

"Where do you have to go?"

"Some place called Hightstown"

"It's not a bad neighborhood. Mostly high up working class to low end upper class. How many of New Jersey kids do you have on your list?"

"Of the Two hundred exchange personnel that we are trying to swap, seven of them are from your fine state."

She held her hand out "Let me see your list. I can probably help you out a little. What are you looking for?"

"I couldn't let you do that."

"Of course you can. What are friends for? Especially when most of the information is a finger click away."

"Well, if you're sure it isn't any trouble. Mostly I have to go to these kids' home and interview their folks, neighbors and friends. See what they were like in school and form a general opinion."

"Pete, my boss, has decided to cut my work load for this week only because he knew I wouldn't take the week off. So how about I work on this list, and flesh out the background a little and I let you take me out to dinner tonight. That is, if you don't have any plans?"

This was going to be easier than he thought.

"Well, Sara if you're sure that it isn't a problem, I would love to let you do my leg work and I'll even let *you* take me out to dinner. But to ease my conscience a little, how about if I pay for it "

She nodded and looked at her own watch. "You know, I've got nothing on my desk that isn't waiting on someone else. How about I drive you out to Hightstown and show you around, introduce you to the Chief of Police and then go over to the high school. And depending on the rest of the list, have dinner?"

"Are you sure? I'd hate to make you my slave for the day."

"Yeah, right. Cat and I had many conversations about you. I think, if I remember correctly, you won a bet with her and she had to be your servant for the weekend? Something about making her wash your socks and underwear by hand."

"She exaggerated. I let her use the machine."

She picked up her phone "Pete? Sara. If you're serious about taking that lost time, I think I'll take you up on it. Yeah, an old friend of mine is in town and I told him that I would show him the sights. Get your mind out of the gutter you pig, or I'll tell Manda how bad you're being, especially in my delicate condition. Yeah, I'll see you in the morning."

Butler/Harry looked at her. "Are you pregnant or sick?"

She shook her head. "No. I just said that to get a rise out of him. I'm sure you read that my ex-husband had kept me locked in the basement for a few days. Well, he also decided to drug me, knock me out and apparently have sex with me. Fucking bastard."

Harry looked down and tried to look a little uncomfortable. "I'm sorry. The article didn't go into details. If you're sure…"

Standing up and taking her purse from the desk drawer she came from around the desk and held the door open for him. "Harry, I was asleep and didn't feel a thing. I was also spared having to go to the arraignment. That was where my boss, Pete is right now. He is handling the charges and the arraignment. We're asking for no bail based on the charges. I'm just glad my sister isn't defending him."

Sara closed her door and motioned for him to precede her. As they walked to the elevator she gave him the back ground on her sister and how she became the opposing council in a major trial. As they headed toward the garage and continued in their conversation, neither was aware that they were being watched and photographed by several different entities.

Chapter 29

Tim continued to look through the files for some clue that would lead to the traitor. He looked at his watch and confirmed it with the clock on the wall. Funny, he thought, how clock bound they all were. His mind turned over to Butler. One minute he was packing it all in and heading home, the next he was out on his own trying to save some bastard princess. It sounded like some contrived Hollywood plot. Butler would have been surprised to know that he knew Sara's real identity. It had taken some major investigating, What had attracted Tim's attention wasn't Sara or her existence. It was a picture of the Prince of Wales in New York city in the late sixties. The picture showed him in a night club with a very pretty Hispanic woman. She looked vaguely familiar. It was during one of his daily checks on Sara that he put two and two together. It was definitely a secret that could rock the Crown. And she was a secret that someone would kill for or die knowing about. It had also shocked him that the Prince had been a stand up guy as far as his illegitimate child was concerned.

Nowadays, the pregnancy would have been terminated the second it had been discovered. The Royals might have played nice before, but Diana ended that.

Tim was one of the few people who had been in on the discussion that Princess Diana shouldn't be allowed to remarry, much less have other children. The argument had been made that any children she had, despite the divorce agreement, would give them a claim to the throne, however slight. Why take any chances? Then suddenly Diana was dead and everyone was claiming that it had been an accident.

Tim regretted that conversation deeply. He always felt that he had been the instigator behind it. Maybe if he hadn't speculated out loud, Diana may still be alive. And while Sara Cohen might be a Yank she was still a Royal and didn't deserve to die an early death. It wasn't her fault that the Prince couldn't keep his trousers zipped.

But all the same, she was a liability while she stayed out in the open. The problem was that one princess dying would be a tragedy, but two dying would be a conspiracy. And just as sure as the Brits liked tea, the truth of her existence would come to light. Tim shook his head. Another princess would not die because of him. He was loyal to the Crown to a fault, but the murder of an innocent was where he drew the line. He picked up another file, not sure of what he was looking for, but sure that once he found it, he would know who the culprits were.

Chapter 30

Butler held the door open for Sara. Exiting the police department had been slow. It seemed that Sara knew everyone and everyone of them stopped her to say how glad they were that she made it out alive. From the Chief to the deputy chief and everyone else in the building, Sara was their friend.

The interview had gone well. As part of his cover, Butler had explained that the British Intelligence was doing a rapid background investigation and while most everything that they needed to know was in the files on the computers, a face to face with local people who knew the volunteers was invaluable.

Only seven names and while the cover story was true, Butler wouldn't usually handle this. But no one here needed to know that. After coffee and stories, Butler gave the files to the Chief along with permission to run an investigation, however brief. So they said their goodbyes and headed out of the building. Half hour later, they were heading to Butler's assigned hybrid. Anyone running the plates would see the diplomatic license and leave him alone. His cover had to be good.

They went to the first address and conducted the interview with the father who was at home. He himself was a disabled veteran and was so proud that his daughter had been selected from all of the volunteers. When they were done with the dad, they went to the neighbors and talked to anyone who answered the door. They talked to the people mowing the lawns, talked to the convenience store owner about the other two selectees as well. It only made sense to cover as much ground as possible.

So far the young lady was well liked, polite and without blemish. No one was home at the other two candidates. But the neighbors in the area were more than happy to talk about the kids and how they were a benefit to the service. Butler knew that this wasn't important in the scheme of things, but it gave him the chance to get to know Sara, to find out what kind of person she was. It was best to know what you might need when dealing with a subject. Too much knowledge was never a bad thing.

They stopped for lunch at a local pizzeria that Sara claimed had the best buffalo wing pizza in the world. Butler looked dubiously at the slices of pizza in front of him. He'd never had buffalo wings, to begin with. He had heard about them, but his curiosity never got the best of him when it came to fad foods. He looked across to Sara who was obviously in some sort of taste bud rapture, if the look on her face was any indication. He gingerly picked up the slice and bit in. Chewing it up for a moment, letting the flavors slide across his tongue, he decided that it wasn't that bad. The bite from the sauce hit the back of his throat and made his eyes water. He hurriedly swallowed and picked up his bottle of iced tea. Not that any self respecting Brit would consider the concoction as "tea". But it did cool the burn in his throat.

"I guess I should have warned you about the kick." She was almost laughing at him, at the very least, her eyes were.

"You have a wicked streak in you, Sara Cohen. Cat warned me about that. I was looking out for plastic spiders and rubber snakes. Who knew that you would attack a man's taste buds in this manner."

Laughing so hard that her sides hurt, the look on his face was worth the guilty pang of her conscious. "You should have seen the look on your face when the burn started. I almost expected steam to come shooting out of your ears." She wiped at the tears that were coming out of the corners of her eyes.

"Ms. Cohen, you have a devil streak in you that your mother should have spanked away in your childhood."

She sobered a bit, at least having the decency to stifle her laugh. "I'm sorry Henry. I couldn't help it. Cat always said that you were a bit stuffy but a good sport. I couldn't resist. But you have to admit, your tongue has never felt so alive."

Butler gave a small smile. "You're right. It was a very unusual experience and not all bad. Is there any way they can tone back the heat so that I could enjoy the flavor?"

She sprinkled a bit of Parmesan cheese on it. "That should cool the fire a bit. Try it now."

He bit into it. The cheese did tone the fire down and he was able to savor the taste. "You know Sara, you might be right. I don't think that I have ever had anything like this before. I don't know if it will replace moo goo gai pan, but I will definitely be on the look out for this later on. You know, London has really caught up with the States as far as pizzerias go. I wonder if I can get this to catch on there?"

Sara nodded as she tore into another slice. "Maybe get a patent or go into business with a pizzeria and serve this. Did you see the other things that Tony has going on back there? Chicken Alfredo pizza, bruschetta pizza, meatball pizza. I'm telling you, American pizza isn't just about sauce and pepperoni anymore.

So, I would suggest that we head on over to the high school next and talk to the staff there and maybe some of the kids that may still be there. The one of the kids on your list graduated at the time that the current seniors were freshman. At the very least, the teachers and counselors stay put. I went by there a few weeks ago and some of my teachers are still there and I graduated twenty years ago."

He popped the last of the crust into his mouth and wiped his mouth. "Good idea. Twenty years ago, huh? That makes you…?"

"Thirty nine on my next birthday."

"Really, you look good for your age."

"Aw, come on, don't tell me you are one of those types that a woman's level of attraction diminishes with her age. I thought you were evolved and all that."

Butler smiled and shot an imaginary gun at her "Gotcha!"

She closed her eyes, "Yeah, you got me. I deserved that. Now, let's go. The school let's out in a couple of hours."

They slid out of the booth and threw out the plates and bottles. Heading to the car, they made small talk, mostly Sara narrating about the area and how it had grown and expanded since she and her family had moved there from Queens. As they headed through the town, Butler was struck by how easy it was to talk to her. A part of him felt a little guilty, that Katey had barely been gone for a half year and here he was talking to a woman and enjoying it, despite his cover.

Sara showed him how to get to the school. One of the things that Butler was sure of was that the town layout hadn't been thought ahead. The streets were just as winding and round about as they were in London.

They parked in the lot in a visitor spot. He was surprised at the number of cars parked in the student parking. What surprised him even more was that for such a rural area, the parking lot boasted everything from the barely held together clunker to more than a few Hummers. There was even a few BMW's and a scattering of Mercedes'. The economic ranges were well represented if the kid's cars were any judge.

Even the school building was ultra modern. As they entered, a uniformed police officer greeted them at the door

93

and directed them to the security booth twenty yards to the right. So, Butler thought. They kept an armed cop inside the school and the security booth was enclosed in bullet proof glass and it was obvious from Sara's small talk as she logged them in that the guard was most likely a retired cop. Interesting.

Further examination impressed Butler. There were security gates at each intersection that would come down and secure that particular hallway and cut it off from the rest of the school.

They walked to the principal's office down a long corridor. More bullet proof glass. The secretary told them to have a seat and the principal would meet with them as soon as she was off of the phone.

"Sara" Butler quietly said as they sat down "I couldn't help but notice that this school is more secure than some government offices that I've been to."

She gave a rueful nod "Yeah, after all of the school shootings, most of the schools consulted with security and anti-terrorist building designers, ours included. All of the schools that were built in the sixties and seventies were pretty much demolished and rebuilt with those designs in mind. The principal and the security booth can drop anyone of those gates at any time. The classes have been redesigned with blind areas that a gunman cannot get a clear shot into. And as an extra precaution, the schools periodically run drills similar to fire drills. If a particular code is called the kids practice going into the blind area and huddling down. It's sad, but necessary."

Butler was shocked. He had been in the business so long that he was both impressed and saddened by the fact that terrorism had breached the sanctity of childhood.

It was his turn to give a rueful nod "I remember when I was a kid that we would hold those bomb drills, the one where you hid under your desk when the air raid siren went of…"

"I remember those. Like hiding under a desk was going to stop a ton of concrete from bashing your head in."

"Yeah. But at least it was giving us a false sense of doing something. Do you think those drills will help?"

Sara shrugged "Who knows, but like the bomb drills, it's better than nothing." Peering through the window, she saw what she assumed was the principal hang up the phone. After a minute, the woman looked out of the window and motioned for them to come in. Butler followed Sara into the office, taking the time to appreciate her shape. He mentally slapped himself. It was never a good idea to allow yourself to be attracted to a potential target. They both had a seat while introductions were made.

Sara was all smiles, like she was seeing an old friend. She was as it turned out. "Ms. Cutler. I don't know if you remember me, but I had you for my ninth grade government."

"As a matter of fact, I do remember you. I use you as an example of what overcoming adversity will do." She looked over to Butler "Sara here is the epitome of ADHD. Of course, back then we didn't have a label for it, but she was a text book case. And now she is a lawyer and a prosecutor. I couldn't have been more pleased if she were my own child. So what brings you to your alma mater?"

"Besides a trip down memory lane and an ego boost? I don't know if you have heard, but an Armed Forces Service Member exchange will be taking place between the US and Great Britain. And seven New Jerseyans have been selected to be part of the Great Two Hundred Exchange, fifty from each branch of the service. So, Mr. Marshall here is handling the background interviews to make sure that no one from our great state is going to embarrass us."

"That's fantastic. What an opportunity. So how many of them belong to us?"

"Three. Christina Hodge, Amy Moore and Sean Levinski. I understand that they all were in the same graduating class. What can you tell me about them?"

Mrs. Cutler turned to her computer and after clicking and typing in a few keys, she put on her glasses that had been sitting on her desk. She grinned at them "Sign of my age. I can see for miles but up close, I'm doomed. My husband laughs at me and tells me I either need these glasses or longer arms." That got an appreciative chuckle.

Chapter 31

James read the e-mail from Butler again. A crease formed on his lined forehead and he again questioned his agent's judgment. Granted, the rescue of the princess had been handled better than expected. And making it look as if a local had been behind it had been a stroke of genius, but posing as the brother of an old college mate was really pushing the envelope. His thoughts were interrupted by the buzzer next to his phone indicating that someone was coming in. A small pop-up on his computer screen showed Laraby requesting entry.

She was alone and carrying what he assumed was an empty coffee cup. She was a great agent but her one phobia was dirty coffee cups. Even she thought it was ridiculous, especially since she went on annual field survival qualifications that involved being dropped blindfolded into a wilderness area with nothing but the clothes on her back. She always qualified in a respectable time frame.

What her boss didn't know was that as much as she hated wilderness qualifying, she loved undercover work in equal amounts. She had been selected as his assistant over all other agents, male and female, because of her ability not only to think fast on her feet, but also her talent at being a social chameleon.

She had posed as a hooker, a Saudi princess, a lady in waiting, a secretary and a mechanic. She had a photographic memory, was able to mimic accents and local dialects within seconds of hearing it once and while she wasn't one of the I.T. people, she could keep up hacking with some of the best of them.

Laraby was ambitious. She wanted her boss' job as soon as he retired. And while she was as loyal as the next agent, there was a dark part of her soul that made her think, and even consider, some of the ways to get James to retire early. Ambition could be a bad thing. But it could also be the catalyst that would make someone act out of character, to do something that they themselves would condemn had someone else acted on the impulse. With that thought in mind, she went into James' office, holding her empty coffee cup, ambition burning in her eyes.

Chapter 32

Sara and Butler left the school and headed to her car. They were smiling and chatting like old friends. As they got into her car, Sara's phone rang. She pulled it out of her purse and looked at the number. She looked over at Butler "It's my mom." Opening the phone she hit the send button. "Hi, Ma. What's up?"

"Nothing Sweety. I was wondering if you'd be all right with the girls staying over for the night?"

Shaking her head into the phone, she gave a small smile "Ma, why don't you just spend the night at my house?"

"Because your beds suck and I don't want to haul my mattress pad all over town. And besides, I promised the girls that we could watch the video's from their births and you don't have a VCR."

"You know, we could transfer those over to DVD without a problem."

"And you could let the girls come over for the night. I promise that they will get to school on time and all the homework will be done. It's sad when you make your mother beg, you know."

Sara gave a soft chuckle. "Yeah, but it's fun. Sure the girls can go that huge long distance of across the street to spend the

99

night at your house. I'll drive them to school in the morning. Save you the trip. I love you Mom."

"I know Baby. Enjoy your night. I'll have the girls call before bedtime."

Closing the phone, Sara looked over at Butler. "Well, Harry. Looks like I am free tonight. What time do you have to get back to the consulate?"

"No particular time. I can e-mail these to the ambassador anytime. Since you were here to help, I'm done ahead of schedule….What?"

She had been smiling, almost laughing at him and she shook her head at him. "Nothing. It's just been a while since I talked to Cathy. It was one of the things that was hardest to break her of, that whole 'said-welling' thing. I always told her if you can say "skate" you can properly pronounce "scheduling".

"So, you are the one to blame for my sister's butchering of the English language. We came close to blows when I made fun of the way she sounded like a bloody Yank, you know."

Sara shook her head and put the Jeep into gear. "No, she didn't mention that. So how do you feel about sea-food for dinner?"

"Sounds good to me. And this time, I pay. I'm not some begger."

"Fine by me. Did Cat ever tell you about the time we held a Chinese fire drill in a Chinese restaurant?"

They traveled in comfortable conversation, enjoying each others company, not for an instant did either one have an inkling about what was coming next.

Chapter 33

Tim looked at his computer screen and followed the GPS blip on the map display. Butler was posing as a consulate employee doing background checks on proposed soldier exchanges. Good cover. Not only did it provide a cover, but it was actually getting a job done that MI-6 had been assigned.

Butler didn't know that he had a GPS bug attached to his heel, literally. Just because he was an agent, didn't mean that he was loyal to a fault. Anyone could be bought, and everyone had a price. Who knew what motivated a person. Tim watched as the blip stopped at a restaurant in Cranbury. So they were staying local for dinner. Good. It made keeping an eye on him even easier.

Chapter 34

Butler popped the pill as soon as they finished desert. By the time they reached the car, he was turning a sickly shade of green. Sara pulled over to the side of the road while Butler emptied his stomach. She asked him if he wanted to go to the hospital. Butler shook his head.

"No. Just drop me off at my car and I'll get back to the embassy. They have a doctor on staff there, you know."

"If you're sure?" She was watching him get grayer by the second. Whatever had gotten him was really bad.

"Harry, we're only a couple of blocks from my house. How's about we head there and get you something to settle your stomach. You're in no shape to drive right now."

Butler nodded his head and let out a small moan for effect. The pill he took would empty his stomach, but not really affect him this badly, but he was a good actor.

They pulled into the driveway of Sara's house. Since her garage was behind the house and not visible from the street, they went into the house unobserved. She helped him through the door and into the mud porch. She kicked off her shoes out of habit and walked with Butler leaning on her shoulder over to a chair by the kitchen island.

Good thing the chair had a back, she thought as Butler laid his head back against the cool wood. She filled the teapot with water and looked over at him. He was still green around the gills and his face was ashen. Suddenly, he popped his eyes open and looked around frantically. Anticipating what was coming, Sara pointed to the mud porch that they had just come through. "Door's on the right". He ran past her and slammed the door open, just in time to retch and heave into the toilet.

This went on for a few minutes while the teapot boiled. Hearing the water in the sink running and the sound of gargling, Sara assumed that the worst was over for a few minutes. She put a ginger teabag in a cup to steep and got a cup out for herself. A nice chamomile to help her relax.

He half staggered-half walked back to the chair that he had so suddenly vacated. Sitting back, he really got into the part. "Just a few minutes and I should be fine. I am so sorry about this. I don't know what I ate, but it certainly didn't agree with me."

"You're right about that. Here, I made you some ginger tea. It works pretty good on what ails you." He took the mug from her and let the steam hit his face. He loved ginger tea, even when he wasn't sick. He took a cautious sip. She had put in a dash of honey. Nice touch. He closed his eyes and let it slide down his throat. Even though he wasn't really ill, vomiting did roughen up the throat a bit. The tea helped.

"And another thing, Harry. You're staying in my guest room tonight. There is no way I am letting you get behind the wheel of a car in your condition. You may not have been drinking, but in my opinion, you are just as impaired as if you had. And besides, Cath would have my ass if anything happened to you after you left here."

Exactly as he planned! "I couldn't impose…" he began.

Holding up a hand to stop the inevitable argument that she knew was what politeness required "Harry, knock it off.

The guest room is already for someone and it's no trouble. It even has it's own bathroom, so if you need to hurl again, you won't have to travel too far for the toilet . So, drink some more tea and hopefully your last technicolor art work was just deposited into the sewer system."

He took a few more sips then stood up. He let himself sway a bit so that Sara felt compelled to reach out a hand to steady him.

"This is so embarrassing." He said.

"Nonsense. I've seen your sister worse than this. Not too mention myself. I'm sure she told you about spring break in Panama City."

"I'm sure she did, but after all of the other exploits, please refresh my memory."

"How about I give you all the gruesome details tomorrow on our way back to the office? Do you need help getting undressed or can you handle this alone?"

"I should be alright with that. And thank you, Sara. You're right. Driving like this would have been foolish."

"Anytime. I almost never get to be the knight in shining armor. So this is a real good karma thing for me. If you need anything, holler. I'm a pretty light sleeper."

And I'm an even lighter sleeper, he thought as she closed the door left the room. He listened as she walked down the hall and ascended up the stairs. He could see her in his mind as she went into her room and walked into the bathroom. He undressed to his boxers and undershirt while she brushed her teeth and did whatever else her nighttime routine was.

He felt a stab in his heart as he remembered his own Katey's bedtime rituals. She always took off her makeup, brushed her teeth then moisturized. One time he remarked about the routine to her, how it never varied. She had laughed at him, saying that only he would notice something like that. He knew it wasn't true. It was in his training. But it made her feel special that he would memorize her habits, so he had let it go. Turning down the comforter, he slid into the cool sheets. One thing about Sara, she did appreciate her beddings and linens. It spoke volumes about her. He turned off the light and slipped into a light slumber. This was better than sleeping in the car, he thought. Much better.

Sara had just gotten into her bed and was reaching for her cell phone when it vibrated. She looked at the number and smiled. "Hi, Mom. I was just getting ready to call you and the girls to say goodnight."

"I know. I saw your t.v. go on and the bathroom light went off, so I figured you were tucked in for the night. And whom, may I ask, is in the guest room?"

"Are you spying on me?"

"Yes, and so what. You were abducted in broad day light, held captive for three days and I'm supposed to just get over that? You're lucky that I'm not in that bed next to you. Which gets us back to the guest room."

"You know, Dad's supposed to be the Jewish yenta, not you."

"Yeah, well I'm Jewish by injection. Now stop evading the question. Talk."

Sara gave a small chuckle. Her mother was relentless and had always been. "Remember Cathy Marshall from grad school?"

"That British girl?"

"Yeah. Her brother is here on assignment and asked for my help. He's checking out some kids from the area that are on a military exchange kind of thing."

"I saw that on t.v. So, why does that mean he has to sleep at your house? Don't they have rooms at the embassy for people like him?"

"Ma, knock it off. I've known Cathy for years. I couldn't kick him to the curb. Especially since he got sick, I mean, hurling chunks out of the car window sick. He looked like hell and I didn't think it would be a good idea for him to drive like that."

"So, is he cute?"

"Ma, I'm not even going to go there. Can I say goodnight to the girls?"

"Well, if you are going to be like that, I suppose."

It was barely a second before her youngest baby, T.J., got on the phone. A full five minutes passed while T.J. told her mother about her day and her latest best friend and how yucky lunch was. Sara closed her eyes and listened to the little girl tell her about all of the little trial and triumphs from her day. She wanted to record this moment and hold it forever. Childhood was so short, there was barely enough time to appreciate how precious and wonderful it was before the next stage of life kicked in and there were different joys to appreciate.

After blowing kisses into the phone, Cassidy came on. Clearly she had been pushing at

T. J. to get off of the phone, insisting that it was her turn.

"Hi Baby Girl. What's the hurry? I thought you were going to take T.J.'s head off."

"Mom, you remember the play that I tried out for. I got the lead! I beat out Brittany Davis. I out sang and out acted her fat butt. It wasn't even a contest. She always goes around thinking she's all that, but I stomped all over her!"

"Way to go, princess! Like there was a doubt. I knew you were so much better than she could hope to be."

Sara listened as Cassidy recounted not the audition results, but the rival's reactions. There was something about teenage girls that was so much more dramatic than any soap opera could ever be.

"So other than kicking Brittany's butt all over the stage, how did that math test go?"

"Uhm…"

"Uhm, is not what I was looking for, Cass."

"Would it help to say that I did the best that I could and considering the circumstances, I think I did really good."

"Did well, not good. And how well?"

"A C plus. We had to rework the ones we got wrong as homework. Grandma helped and so did Uncle Steve."

"I'm glad. As long as you learned from your mistakes."

"Mom, did you watch the news today?"

Here it comes, Sara thought. "I didn't but I imagine you did."

"Yeah. You and Dad were the leading story. Grandma didn't know that I watched it, but it was pretty hard to miss, 'specially when it was all over every channel and on the radio."

"I bet. So, is this something we handle on the phone, or do you want to come home and talk?"

"I think it can wait. But I need to know, do you hate him?"

She sighed deeply then took a deep breath. "Cassie, I don't hate him. I feel sorry for him, I feel pity for him, but I don't hate him. And even if I did, it doesn't- nor will it ever affect how I feel about you and your sister. I love you and I always will, regardless of your father's actions. I think I'm mature enough to know that one has nothing to do with the other. Is that what you wanted to know?"

She heard the girl smile into the phone. "yeah, I guess that's what I needed to hear. I love you Mom."

"I love you too, mijita. Now get yourself to bed and I will drive you to school in the morning."

"Goodnight" Cassidy said and clicked off the phone. Sara closed her's and put it back on the nightstand charger.

She had the t.v. on mute but turned it up when she saw her picture on the screen. The anchor was outlining the story then turned the monitor over to a reporter who had been at the courthouse for the arraignment.

Listening intently, she watched as her ex-husband was led into the courtroom dressed in jailhouse orange. Anger flooded her heart and her head as she watched him. A litany of foul language bubbled into her mouth. She picked up a softball that she kept by the side of the ball and threw it with all of her might at the far wall. It hit with a dull thud and fell to the ground. Sara had thrown that ball at that part of the wall so often that she had eventually put a soft patch there to absorb most of the force.

Turning off the t.v., she was now thoroughly disgusted. The bastard had pled "not guilty." Far as she was concerned, it was an open and shut case. If the Camden County Prosecutor blew this one, she would personally nail his balls to the courthouse door. She reached up and turned off the bedside light, not seeing Butler standing at the side of the door, checking on her.

Chapter 35

The thud of the softball hitting the wall had propelled him out of the bed and silently up the stairs, gun in hand. Once he satisfied himself that she was all right, he watched her turn off the light and lay down. He stood there until he heard her breathing return to normal then fall into a sleep rhythm. Silently, he padded down the stairs and back to his room once again grateful that he was not in a cold cramped car. All surveillance should be this nice.

Chapter 36

The vibrating of her phone woke Sara with a start. She grabbed it and looked at the number. Not recognizing it, she hit the send button and answered groggily. "This better be important."

"Sara, it's Cathy. Are you all right? I just read what happened. I can't believe that asshole. You should have let me kill him while I had the chance."

"Cat?! I thought you were on safari? How did you hear about me?"

"Satellites, silly. I bring my computer with me everywhere. Did I wake you?"

"You know damn well you did. You'll never guess who is in my guest room right now?"

"I'll bite. Who?"

"Your brother. He's here on some assignment with the consulate and got sick when we went to dinner, so I made him stay with me. Isn't that a riot?"

"Sara, listen to me very carefully. Get out of the house."

Suddenly, Sara was fully awake and reaching into her night table for her 9mm that she kept in the drawer. "What's up, Cathy?"

"Sara, Harry is here with me. He joined me yesterday as a surprise."

Her blood ran cold. "Cathy, I'm calling the police. Bye, I'll call you later."

Turning on the light, she nearly jumped out of her skin when she saw Butler at the door. She dropped her phone and trained the gun on his chest.

"So, I guess I need to explain who I am."

Chapter 37

The nurse at the Camden County Correction Center was always on the look-out for ways to make extra money. And this was very lucrative.

All he had to do was give Inmate Peterson a little extra something in his juice. The nurse didn't care what it was. He was assured that it was untraceable and that the effects of the juice wouldn't be known for some time.

And after what this creep had pulled, the nurse would have done it for free.

Chapter 38

Shaking her head, she pushed buttons on the phone and was hitting "send" when he knocked the phone from her hand and hit her wrist, forcing her to drop the gun. It was done in one swift move, followed by him knocking her back onto the bed. She tried to scramble to the other side, but he straddled her and pinned her hands over her head with one hand and clamped his other hand over her mouth. She was kicking and trying to buck him off.

"Stop for half a second and I'll let you up. Sara, now! Calm down and I will let you up. Consider, I was standing at your door and if I had meant to do you any harm, I would have by now. I'm going to let you up, then I want you to call your parents and ask them to come over. They are part of this. All right?"

Sara looked him in the eyes. Something there told her that he was being honest, despite having her pinned and pretty much at his mercy. She nodded and he slowly released his hand. Sitting up he looked at her warily. He half expected a punch in the groin and was ready for it. He got off of her and handed her the bedside phone. She took it from him and dialed her mother's number, never taking her eyes from his.

"Ma, can you and Daddy come over, right now? No, leave the girls asleep, just come over."

Standing next to the door, Butler had retrieved the gun, unloaded it and had taken it apart. He motioned for her to precede him "I suggest that we go down and put on a pot of coffee. You're going to need it."

They were hitting the landing when her parents rushed in. They had keys to all of their children's houses just in case of an emergency. They both were still in their pajamas and slippers. Barry had a baseball bat and Maria was sporting a shotgun. IF Sara hadn't been so scared, she would have thought the scene funny.

Maria raised the gun to her shoulder and aimed it at Butler. "Who the fuck are you, pendejo?"

He held his hands up and looked at the older woman "What is it with woman and guns in this family. Mrs. Cohen. I mean no harm to your daughter. As a matter of fact, I am here to protect her. If you could kindly put your gun down, I will explain everything."

Dubiously, both of the Cohen's followed Sara and Butler toward the kitchen. Silently, Sara started the pot of coffee and everyone took a seat. While the coffee brewed Sara joined them. "It's going to be a few minutes. So, would you kindly explain who the hell you are."

"My name is Special Agent Butler. I am with Her Majesty's service, MI-6."

Barry looked shocked "You mean, like that James Bond crap?"

Butler gave a small grin "Something like that. I was sent here to investigate Ms. Cohen's disappearance and achieve her recovery."

It was Sara's turn to be shocked. "Why the hell would the Brit's care about me?"

"I think that Mrs. Cohen is going to have to explain that. Madame?" He said to Maria, pointedly.

Her mother got up and went to the liquor cabinet over the stove and pulled out a bottle of Irish whiskey. Silently, she pulled down coffee mugs from the cupboard and pulled the pot out from under the brewer spout and replaced it with each mug, swapping them as they filled. She also poured a generous helping of the whiskey into each one except for Butler's. As she passed out the mugs, she looked at Sara. "We're going to need this."

Taking a sip, Sara wrinkled her nose and added some sugar from the bowl on the lazy Susan.

Barry added some sugar to his, then some more. The coffee was really strong, especially since he wasn't a coffee drinker by habit.

Maria looked at her cup really hard and took a deep breath. "Sara, remember how I always told you that your birth father lived far away and had responsibilities that he couldn't leave, no matter how much he loved us?"

"Yes. I also remember thinking that he couldn't have loved us very much since I never heard from him. And besides, Daddy has always been the best father a kid could have. But what has this got to do with anything."

"What I didn't tell you was who your father was or rather is. Do you remember his name on your birth certificate?"

"Of course. I thought it was strange that a man from England would have a hyphenated name, but who knows with Brits."

"Do you remember his first name?"

"Yes. Why...Oh no! Mom, are you saying that THE Prince is my birth father?"

"He was here in the states, studying for a year before he had to go to the Royal Navy. We fell in love and I got pregnant with you. He insisted that his name be on the birth certificate and he was even there in the delivery room for your birth. He insisted that all Royal births must be witnessed by someone from the Royal family. Shortly after you were born, his father came to New York and insisted that the Crown could not handle another abdication and he must return home to his duties. And even though he loved us both, I knew he couldn't stay. Not without jeopardizing everything that his mother had worked for. So I sent him away. He made sure that you were taken care of financially, but it was agreed by everyone that you would be kept ignorant of your status. There was no point in telling you since you would not be in line of succession."

Sara took a long drink of the coffee. She got up and took the phone off of the base and returned to the table. Dialing the phone to the last number that called her, she got Cathy.

"Hey, sweety. I just wanted you to know that I'm o.k. and I'll tell you all of the details later. I can't tell you everything right now. I promise I am all right and that I am satisfied that the guy pretending to be Harry is not going to kill me. I'll call you back in a couple of hours." Pressing the "off" button she leaned it against her head. Then she looked back at Butler. "So how do you fit into all of this?"

"A daily check has been done on you since the day you were born. As a member of the Royal family, your safety has to be insured at all times. When you dropped off the face of the earth, an alert was made by the local office and I was dispatched to locate and recover you. Once that recovery was made, I was supposed to return to England.

Unfortunately, someone hacked into the files in the medical department and some records were accessed, specifically, the DNA information. So, it was decided that I would stay here and keep you under close watch until we either catch the person who was behind the theft or we can control the outcomes. You, my dear Sara are about to be outed unless we can figure out who the hacker was and what they intend to do with this information."

Sara shrugged. "So the Prince has a love child. Big deal. It was the sixties. It isn't as if I could be of any real consequence outside of my little sphere of reality."

Butler set his cup down. "I beg to differ with you, your Highness. But since your father decided to legitimize you by putting his name on your birth certificate, you are a Royal and therefore you are not only of consequence as you put it, but you are also a liability.

Embarrassment aside, you could be used as a pawn. In case you missed the BBC, the Muslims in the UK are protesting our involvement in Iraq and your younger half brother is also vocal about our involvement and wants us to pull out of the conflict. Along side of that, there is also a rumored plot against the line of succession. There are some who think that The Prince should abdicate in favor of his oldest son. Your existence could be used to black mail him into doing just that."

"I thought Parliament controlled the country."

"Just as your senate controls your country, the president still has the last word."

"So why do you believe that I am in danger. Or am I? Seriously, my existence can be explained away. Documents can be changed. It's not like I want to be queen or anything like that."

He let out a slightly exasperated sigh. "Your Highness…"

Sara held up her hand. "Will you please stop calling me that? I'm not a Royal highness and although I pretended I was some kind of princess when I was a little girl, that is hardly the case now."

"Actually, when the Prince put his name on the dotted line, so to speak, you became a Royal Highness. You are even in the Queen's will as well as the Prince's. And while you are somewhat correct in the fact that you are not likely to become Queen, it is not far from the imagination as history has shown. While you are not in direct line, you and your children are in the lineage. If the first two Princes die without issue, you are next in line through your father."

She looked at him as if he had lost his mind. "Uh, granted I am a little ignorant of British history and all that stuff, but exactly how does this succession thing work? I thought that my parents would have to married to EACH other for me to inherit."

Butler shook his head in the way that suggested he was dealing with a dullard and begging for patience. "Back when Henry the 8th kicked out the catholic church and made his own, he also made a law saying that any child that he and future British monarchs deemed legitimate were such. The Prince insisted that you be declared legitimate. And while the Queen could have fought him on it, he pretty much extorted your legitimization by threatening to abdicate to his younger brother. Her Royal Highness felt that the UK couldn't handle yet another American causing problems with the Crown. Not too mention that the Parliament was already up to it's armpits in it own problems, something like this could fracture the whole foundation. So you were allowed to be acknowledged as an heir to the throne."

Sarah sat back in the chair and contemplated her coffee mug. Then she looked over at her parents. "Did you both know about this?"

They both silently nodded their heads. It was Maria who broke the silence. "Your father and I had been madly in love, but you had to remain a close secret. When Daddy and I got married, Daddy had to be brought into the loop. If God forbid, something happened that would require you to go to England, he deserved to know."

Barry reached over and took her hand into his. "I always said you were a princess. You just didn't know that I meant it literally. Doesn't change anything, though. You are still my little girl, regardless of whose name is on the certificate."

Chapter 38

The computer monitor cast an eerie light into the room. It also gave Laraby an almost alien, malevolent look. She was so intent on the monitor that the vibrating of her phone on her waist band irritated her. She checked her watch.

The Director would be in the building in ten minutes. She had his car wired to send her phone a signal when he started his car. And as most older people tended to be, he was as predictable as the train schedule.

He would walk out of his house, get the mail at his front door, pull up to a newspaper hawker, roll down his window and hand him a coin, get his paper, roll up the window then drive to the building. Park his car in his spot, get out, get his briefcase from the back seat, walk into the building and greet the guard at the counter. He would then walk through the metal detector archway and take the stairs the four flights up to his office.

Any more predictable and she would know what time he went to the loo. Matter of fact, she did. What surprised her the most was that the Director had been a field agent and a damn good one in his day. But life got soft and turned him soft, making him forget his training. Something that she capitalized on.

She had been working all night on the project. It was imperative that it come from the Director's computer and security as tight as it was meant that she couldn't do a remote hack into the system. After this, she would be considered a hero to the Crown.

Chapter 39

While Sara was embracing her parents after the revelation of her true parentage, Butler's blackberry vibrated in his pocket. He pulled it out and touched the button to open his messages. It was an e-mail from the director indicating that he needed to open a secure e-mail. Puzzled, Butler went up to his room where his computer was.

The unit was small enough to fit into a pocket on cargo pant but was powerful enough to handle everything he needed including his encryption system.

After getting a secure link, he logged on and stood by for a retina scan, followed by a thumb print. It seemed a bit much, but considering everything he had to deal with, one couldn't be too careful.

He read the message. Had the old man lost his freaking mind?! He examined the message. Everything was in order. He ran a scan and backed traced the message. It had definitely come from the Director's computer. But something was wrong with the message. He couldn't put his finger on it, but something wasn't right with the message.

And why would the Director send this in an e-mail? An order like this had to be face to face or at least on the phone. Butler shook his head. Yes, this order had been a possibility, but it was supposed to be used as a last resort. this message made it sound as matter of course in events. And this even gave a date that the termination was to take place by. The Director knew better than anyone that you couldn't do a high profile hit by a specific date and make it look like an accident. What was he thinking?

Well, there was no way he was going to take out a Royal, even a bastard Royal, without a confirmation. That happened once, and people were still questioning it ten years later. He pulled out his phone and dialed the Director's office. Oddly, he got a voice mail message saying that the Director was on vacation. What was going on?

Chapter 40

Laraby saw that Butler had downloaded his messages and as she predicted, he dialed the Director's office number. She had programmed the phones to divert all in-coming calls to an automated answering system that said the Director was on vacation. She had even programmed the system to make it sound like the Director's voice. Clever. And if she was correct, Butler's next call would be to her. As if on cue, her cell phone rang. Caller I.D. showed Butler's number. This was going easier than she thought.

She hit the button to accept the call. "Yes, Butler."

"Laraby, is everything all right with the Director?"

"Yes, as far as I know. He's in his office right now."

"Odd. I tried calling his number and was sent to his voice mail. Could you physically check him and have him call me?"

"Surely. Is something wrong?"

"Yes. There is and I need to clarify an instruction I received."

Laraby pretended to hesitate for a second.

"Butler, now that you've called, maybe you should be made aware of the Director's, how should I put this? As of late, the Director hasn't really been himself. Giving contradictory

123

statements, forgetting things he's requested. He's formed behavior habits that at first I dismissed as human behavior but have taken on an almost obsessive quality. Just yesterday, he ordered his car to take him home, only to go down to the garage and drive himself home."

She could hear him rub his hand across his face. "Why are you telling me this, Laraby? I'm ten thousand miles away."

"I'm just saying that maybe it's time to send the old man to the pasture. You are the closest thing he has to a friend. I hate to say this, but maybe his age is getting to him."

"Well, that would answer my question about the e-mail I received."

"Something in particular?"

"Matter of fact, he instructed me to terminate my current assignment."

"As in...?"

"Yes. I thought it odd that he would send that instruction in an e-mail and I wanted a verbal confirmation."

She grinned broadly for just a split second. She didn't want to tip her hand, especially to Butler. The man was almost psychic when it came to his job.

"It was definitely a good call to phone in to verify the message. Is there any harm in delaying the order a day or two?"

"Not that I can see. The press hasn't gotten wind of Sara, other than her kidnapping and subsequent rescue." He purposely left out that his cover had been blown and that she was aware of her parentage. That was one bridge that he wold cross when necessary.

"Let me have a moment with this, Butler. Even the Director cannot take out a member of the Royals without the Queen's authorization. The next message you get from me will be either go or stop. This way you know that I've checked it out. Any way that you can send, me that e-mail."

This caught Butler by surprise. Suddenly, alarms began going off in his head. Something wasn't quite right. "Uhm. Yeah. I'll forward it to you right now."

Laraby could hear the soft clicking of the computer keys. This was even easier than she had thought it would be. "All right, I've got it. I'll get back to you shortly." With that, she disconnected the call.

By this time next week, she would be the interim Director and well on her way to the permanent Director, all before she was forty five.

Chapter 41

Butler went back to the message. There was something off, just a little, but he couldn't put his finger on it. James had been his friend for more years than either cared to remember. It was hard enough to accept the loss of time much less to be witness to the ravages it made. But James? Butler gave a mental shake. Not James. Something was definitely afoot, he just wasn't sure how to prove it. At least not yet.

Chapter 42

Sara watched him as he left the room. He was definitely easy to watch both coming and going. She turned back to her parents and gave a blush when she was busted appreciating the Brit's backside.

"O.K. so I like to look. I'm not a nun you know"

Maria smiled. "You don't have to defend yourself to me. He's hot. Not as hot as Daddy, but he is something."

Barry leaned over to kiss his wife's cheek. "You're sweet, but we both know you're full of crap. And if you say he's hot, then he must be. Not that I'm worried about it. I have something that he will never have."

"Your dashing good looks and wonderful kisses?" She asked him coyly.

He chuckled "That and I know where all of your favorite message spots are."

Sara loved to watch her parent's banter. They were the rock that she built her life on. And now, after this revelation, she felt that rock was just a little less stable. Not rocked out from under her, but still a little shaken.

She looked up at the clock on the wall. The girls would be getting up in a few minutes and would be scared that no one was there.

"How about you guys head home before the girls get up and I'll get ready for work? I've got arraignments this morning and I'm supposed to meet with the sheriff. He's running for reelection and figures if he makes nice-nice with all of the D.A.'s that we might throw in for him."

"And are you?" Barry was a big political hound. He could talk politics and conspiracy theories with the best of them. Many arguments and debates at the family dinner table had finely honed Sara's abilities to argue and see more than one side of a position.

Shaking her head, she got up from the table and tightened the belt of her robe. "No, the guy's a schmuck. I don't know what devil he had to sell his soul to to get elected, but I can't see it going for another term."

As she moved toward the stairs, her mother gently grabbed her arm and looked up at her. "Honey I know that this has been a lot to process and I hope you aren't too angry that we kept this from you."

Looking down in her mother's eyes, Sara knew she could never fault this woman. No matter what, Maria had always put her family first. And this time was no different. Whatever anger had been building in her heart melted. Sara knew that no matter what, her parents had her best interests at heart.

"Mom...never in all of my life could I hold a grudge against you. I know that whatever you did, it was because you love me and could never intentionally hurt me."

She knelt down on the floor and hugged the older woman tightly. It was in those arms that Sara knew that no matter what, she was loved by someone for no other reason than just because she was. Kissing her mother's cheek reassured the older woman that all was forgiven. Smiles and friendly jibes released everyone from the room to start the day.

Chapter 43

The computer screen was on a live video feed. The screen was split into four different views. One view was the living room in Sara's house. Another was from her empty office. The other was the front of the school that the girls attended. The last view was from the dome light in Sara's car. It gave him the view from just over her shoulder, including a view of the GPS as well as whatever she was seeing. It gave the advantage of being a fly on the wall. It was all coming together.

The pick-up was going to be the hard part. Getting rid of the guards that had been assigned to cover the kids wasn't all that difficult. The really hard part was getting rid of Butler. At least diverting him long enough to put the plan into action. He smiled as he watched them get up from the table and get on with the day.

Looking at the time display on his computer and checking it against his watch, he was satisfied that everything was on schedule.

Using the mouse he clicked onto another window. After entering a few keys, he checked the balance on his account. The money had been deposited. It was enough to cover his debt and then some. Maybe this time, he would be able to get help for his problem. They say that you have to hit rock bottom before you decide that you are ready to quit. Well, he came to the conclusion that kidnapping a woman and her two children was definitely rock bottom. And while it was an honorable endeavor to protect the innocent, it was his life that was in danger of being lost. He was not an honorable man.

Chapter 44

Laraby knocked on the office door and waited for a response. Funny, she thought. I am about to change the entire M.I.-6 organization and the Prince was going to be the unwitting instrument.

"Come in"

She opened the door and let herself in. His Royal Highness was sitting behind a large wooden desk reading papers that were strewn across the desk. For such a powerful man, one would think that he would be better organized, Laraby mused.

He looked up to her. "Yes Laraby? I don't recall an appointment."

Stepping forward she nodded at him. "I apologize for coming in like this, Sir. But something has come to my attention that I wanted to confirm before it is carried out."

His Highness sat back and put his pen down. "This is highly irregular. Shouldn't you be going to your boss about things?"

"Ordinarily, I would agree, but this is too important and extremely urgent. I'll be blunt, Sir. Did you order the sanction of your daughter?"

The Prince jumped up. "Are you out of your mind?! What are you talking about?! That sanction was to be a last resort! And how the bloody hell do you know about Sara?!"

Laraby congratulated herself on not jumping. The Prince was an incredibly controlled man, not prone to outbursts. Hearing him shout was something for the record books.

"Sir, the Director decided that as his deputy, I should be involved on all things concerning the security and safety of the Royal family, including the family members abroad. That is why I am here. I was contacted by Agent Butler a short time ago. He was requesting verification that his coverage was done and that the job, your daughter and her children, were to be terminated. He informed me that this was done via e-mail and that when he called the Director to verify the instruction, he got the Director's voice mail. I checked on the Director immediately and he was on the phone talking to his son about fishing when he retires. Sir, I'm not one to go behind the Director's back, but before Butler carries out this sanction, I want to hear it directly from you, that you signed off on this."

The Prince had sat back down. Rubbing his palms together, it was clear that his mind was working mile a minute. He stopped rubbing and looked her in the eye.

First this thing with his son and that Al-Qaeda slut and now this. Life was definitely getting way too interesting for him to be comfortable with. "Deputy Laraby. I am grateful that you did go behind the Director's back. Just so that we are clear, I did not approve the sanction against my daughter or her children. As a matter of fact, I want it made clear, short of screaming it to the press, that Sara is to be protected at all costs, my Mother be damned. Do you understand?"

Laraby fairly snapped to attention. "Yes, Sir."

"Please contact Agent Butler and relay those instructions immediately. Dismissed."

She walked out and closed the door as the Prince was picking up his phone and punching a button. It was a short walk to her office and didn't take her long to get there. If anyone had taken the time to look into her eyes, they would see the triumph glinting there. It was with no small satisfaction when she dialed Butler's number. Time to ride in and save the Princess. If things went according to plan, this time tomorrow, Laraby would be interim Director and James wouldn't know what hit him.

Chapter 45

Tim's phone chirped on his belt. He pulled it out and looked at the number. This could not be good. Flipping it open "Mack. Go."

"Mack. I have a courier coming to you. Meet him at the electronics store on the corner of Houston and 42nd. He'll be waiting for you."

The line went dead. Tim closed his phone and was already on his feet heading to the door. He was going alone. That in and of itself wasn't unusual. What was out of the ordinary was that he grabbed his back-up weapon from the drawer before walking out.

The courier was waiting at the counter pretending to look at digital cameras. He was fairly ordinary looking, but as a regular courier, Tim knew him. Courier was just another term for informant, but once they reached courier status, they were considered extremely reliable and their information was worth every dime they asked for.

The shop was small and extremely cramped. There was a banner outside of the store, proclaiming that is was going out of business and everything must go. The place had been going out of business for three years, but it was a good place to get things and to meet someone. Since it was on the tourist strip, the people coming and going were of little interest. Tim pretended to look at cameras next to the courier. The shop was so small that a person could stand at one counter and lean over the opposite counter with no problem. In such a cramped area, It was fairly easy to make an exchange unnoticed. Tim barely felt the flash drive drop into his hip pocket. Since the courier had received his electronic payment before he even left his left apartment, all Tim had to do was walk away.

He got into his car and pulled out his hand held computer. Turning it on and engaging the electronic shield took very little time.

Inserting the flash drive, he scanned it for bugs and viruses. The computer screen told him it was clean.

Opening the file and engaging the encryption file, he first looked at the pictures then read the documents that had been included. It was enough to make Tim lift his eyebrows in shock and surprise. It took a lot to shock him.

Firing up the engine and throwing the car into gear, he got back to the Brownstone in record time. He slammed the door on the way in and hit the security button for the computer room. Sitting down at his desk Tim pushed the intercom button that would summon the unit to the room. None of the computer geeks were there.

"Good" he thought "The less people that knew about this, the better."

Within a few seconds, all the members of the Team had assembled and were curiously looking at their leader.

"Well, chaps. We are up to our willies in it now. I have a confirmed hit list for the Royals and from all indications, it looks as if it was brought about by the Heir. The crews back home are securing everyone even as we speak. Our job is to get Sara and her kids and move them to a secured area. Has anyone heard from Butler lately?"

One of the computer techs answered. "Yeah, Mack. His phone has him at the Cohen residence. matter of fact, he was there all night."

This information was noted by a few raised eyebrows.

"You don't say. Interesting but convenient. Spike, notify the airstrip to have the jet ready to go. Riggins, gather a detail and meet me at the Cohen's. I'll contact Butler. I want to be airborne in three hours. Let's move.

As the unit left en mass, Tim called Butler. It rang once and was immediately answered.

"Hey, Mack."

"Butler, we have a problem."

"Yeah, I know."

"How the hell do you know? I just found out myself."

Butler was confused. "Are we talking bout the same thing?"

"I don't see how. Listen Butler. I just got Intel that has a hit on the entire succession line. We have been ordered to gather and relocate all of them until this thing can be handled. I have sent the crew to secure Sara and the kids. We will be at the landing strip in under an hour. Can you have Sara there by then?"

"Mack. Get in the car and meet me here at Sara's. We have a bigger problem."

"I'm already on my way."

It was Mack's turn to be confused. Things were not going according to plan. Not at all.

Chapter 46

Sara was finishing her makeup and keeping one eye on the clock. She was due in court in two hours. With just enough time to get to the office, check messages, grab her files and go.

The jury had requested further information from the Prosecutor's office. It seemed that Amanda's argument about the baby's existence may have turned a few of the jurors. And even Phil's compelling closing statement hadn't been enough to erase reasonable doubt.   Sara needed this like a hole in the head.

A knock on the door was followed by the door being flung open and Cassidy throwing herself across the bed. She had on her uniform and her hair was up. One thing that Sara insisted upon was that the girls have their hair pulled back. One of her pet peeves was watching someone with long hair twirl it around their fingers. It made her feel like she was watching an act of disinterest, ignorance or nervousness. Her Dad had always said "Don't let them see you sweat". Hair twirling was letting them see you sweat. She knew it was silly, but some things just stay with you.

Stepping into her pumps and adjusting her jacket, she looked in the free standing mirror in the corner of the room.

Making eye contact with her daughter's reflection, she smiled at her. "I see you are all ready. Books packed, lunch money in your pocket, etcetera, etcetera?"

"Yeah. Can I go over to Stephanie's after school today. Her dad is picking her up after school and then we can watch that new 3-D movie on Disney channel."

Shrugging and turning around to face her older child "I don't see why not. Tell Grandma that I said it was o.k. I should be home before dinner. Come on. Let's get moving."

As they went down the stairs, Butler came out of his room. Everyone stopped at the bottom landing. Cassidy's eyes nearly popped out of her head as she took a step back behind her mother.

"Oh, Cass. I am so sorry. This is Mr. Butler. He is a friend of Aunt Cathy's from England. He was out here doing some work and I invited him to stay here instead of driving back to the city last night. I had forgotten he was in the guest room. Mr. Butler, this is my oldest daughter Cassidy. T.J. is in the kitchen. Want to join us for a cup of coffee?"

Butler held out his hand to Cassidy. "It's a pleasure to make your acquaintance. And I would be honored of your company for coffee. But I must beg a moment alone with your mother, if you wouldn't mind?"

Sara looked at Butler with a lifted brow. "Something wrong?"

"Matter of fact, there is."

"Cass, honey. Go pour me a cup and tell T.J. that we will be leaving in twenty minutes, ok.?" She kissed the to of the girl's head as she went past her.

After Cassidy had gone down the hallway and out of ear shot, Sara looked at him expectantly.

"An MI-6 team leader will be here shortly. He received a communique that has put a hit on all of the entire line of succession. You and the girls are to be immediately relocated and taken to a safe location until this situation is cleared up."

All of the color drained from her face. A second later the color was replaced with the red of intense rage. "Are you fucking nuts?! I will not be going anywhere with you and your team. How credible is this threat and how the hell do they know abut us? Hell! I just found out myself!"

"I did tell you that our system had been compromised and that DNA information had been stolen. That theft was used to identify anyone in the data base and that included you and the girls. Even as we speak, the rest of the Royals and their families are being swept up and secured."

"Do you know who is behind this?"

"We are pretty certain that it is your brother, or half brother I should say. It would seem that he doesn't want G.B.- Great Britain, to be in the war any longer and has a soft spot for the Muslims. He has even taken an Al-Qaeda operative as a girlfriend. We are reasonably sure that he doesn't yet know of her affiliations, but even so, he does have a soft spot for peace. And the only way he can get what he wants is to take out all the resistance to his ascension to the thrown. And your being alive and able to make a claim to the thrown is a threat to what he wants."

"So why don't you just take him out? Or expose him to the press?"

"Like I said, we are fairly certain. And just as we are fairly certain that the Heir is behind this, all of it was done through someone else, this way he has no provable ties to the plan. And without that, it is all speculation. So, our current plan is to safeguard all of the Royals, find the proof we need and have the Prince removed from succession."

"You mean have him killed."

Butler looked her dead in the eye "Yes. It's either that, or you and your girls. Is this a hard decision for you?"

Shaking her head no, she didn't even blink.

Chapter 47

Tim got into the SUV and started the engine. He knew the various routes to Sara's house and decided that it was worth the risk to take the shortest one.

Two blocks from the house, he stopped at a stop sign. A slight sound, barely a whisper made him turn around to look at the back seat. The last thing he saw was the barrel of the silencer on a gun just as it fired. His body slumped forward as the killer reached into Tim's front pocket and pulled out his phone. Hitting the send button, he knew the last call was to Butler. As it rang, the killer dropped the phone into Tim's lap, got out of the car and made his way to the clump of trees that would shelter him as he put his plan into effect.

Chapter 48

————————

Butler looked at his phone. What the fuck? Tim should have been pulling up by now.

Sara was helping the girls pack a quick bag, taking only a change of clothes and one thing of importance. Anything else would be provided for them.

Because an explanation had to be made, the girls had been told that it was a gang related problem and that all of them would be kept safe, but they had to leave immediately.

Sara was on her phone talking to her office. She gave them the excuse that there was a death in the family and she had to leave. Since Phil was up to speed and the jury was still out, there really wasn't too much more that she could do. Her parents had been told but the rest of the family would get some explanation later. Right now, they had to get out.

Chapter 49

Butler hit the send button and heard nothing. He listened closely. Something was wrong. Then he heard a gurgle, a death rattle, like a last breath escaping from a body. He had heard it before. He knew what it was.

"SARA!" He yelled at the top of his lungs. He went into overdrive.

She came down the stairs, closely followed by the two girls. One look at his face scared her. Instinctively she shoved her daughters behind her. "What is it?"

"Something is wrong. We have to assume that you are in imminent danger. I want you and the girls to go down to the basement. If I don't come down there in 5 minutes, get out through the window and drive away. I will find you. Give me your phone." She handed it to him. He put it in his pocket and handed her a credit card that he had pulled out of his wallet.

"This is my late wife's. The pin number is on the back. Use it and buy a throw away phone. Did you see that movie "Enough?" She nodded. "Do what she did in that movie. Find a hole for you and the girls. Trust no one except me."

"Why the hell should I trust you?"

"Because I would die before I let anything happen to one of you. Now go."

Sara ran to the kitchen with the girls on her heels. She ran to the door that led to the basement and quietly opened it, slipped in and slowly, cautiously went down the stairs, turning on all of the lights to illuminate every corner of the finished basement.

She did a quick sweep with her eyes, making sure that they were alone. Motioning for them, she waved the girls in front of her, then turned and looked at Butler one last time, her eyes meeting his. It was in that instant that it hit her that she was in love with him. She quietly shut the door locked the deadbolt on it.

Chapter 50

Butler saw the look on Sara's face as she shut the door. It had hit him in the gut like a punch. His wife had been in the ground for less than a month and here he was in love again. But he couldn't think of that right now.

He was certain that Tim was dead, meaning that Sara had been compromised. He pulled up the GPS locater on his PDA. It showed that Tim's phone was less than a mile from the house.

He looked at his watch and headed to the front door. Opening it he cautiously looked around. Clear. He walked to the garage. Sara's car was in the driveway close to the escape window. As he made his way past the window to the back of the house, he saw her peeking through the window.

The clatter of the garbage can lid made him spin around just as the lid smashed in his face. He staggered backwards and felt the house against his back. He was blinded as the blood flowed into his eyes. Swinging his gun around to where he heard breathing, he tried to fire, but the garbage can lid sliced against his wrist. Butler felt the bone snap and his gun drop from it. The can lid then hit him on the side of the head, dropping him to the ground. As he lost consciousness, the last sound that he heard was Sara yelling for someone to stop. Then life faded to black.

Chapter 51

Laraby sat back in her chair and gave a large, satisfied mental pat on the back. This morning it had been announced that she was the interim director and that Director James was taking a sabbatical for heath reasons. This time next week, she would be confirmed as the permanent Director of MI-6. Life was definitely good. A sharp knock on the door broke her mental party. Show time. "Come in"

"Director, we have a problem." It was one of the computer geeks that was always whining about his work station and the lack of respect that they got from the agents. He was somewhat right and Laraby did respect the tech people. They had saved her ass on more than one occasion. There was also the fact that they had been unwitting participants in her coup.

"What's the problem?"

"The U.S. team has not been able to locate their leader or the agent assigned to handle the family in New Jersey. And we ran a check on the GPS locations for both of them. The signals are stationary and have been for more than ten minutes."

"Are they together?"

"No and the signals are within a meter of each other."

Laraby's mind began to fast forward. This was not good. "Get me the team second on the line."

"Already have. She is on line 3"

Lifting an eyebrow as she lifted the phone, she was surprised that she had been anticipated. "This is Director Laraby, with whom am I speaking?"

"Ma'am. I am agent Riggins. We were prepping for a dust off with the Cohen family when our team leader disappeared. His signal had him within a meter of the target's residence. We dispatched a car to the house and found Agent Mack dead in the front seat of his car and Agent Butler incapacitated at the Cohen residence. Ms. Cohen's car is gone."

Laraby leaned an elbow on her desk and tapped her upper lip for a second. "Is everyone on your team accounted for?" This had to be an inside job. Sara's existence had been too closely guarded for it to be the work of an outsider.

"Yes ma'am. The team had been split up to handle the immediate removal of the Cohen's. Everyone is in their positions."

"How has this been confirmed?"

"By GPS locaters."

"Agent Riggins. I want you to do a visual confirmation. If the agent is not in your sight, plan on him or her being the culprit."

Laraby hung up the phone. She assumed that Butler was on his way to the hospital. Hell of a first day. One agent dead, one in the hospital and three Royals missing and presumed kidnapped. The only good thing out of this whole thing was that Sara and her children were of more value alive than dead. She looked up. The tech was standing by the door waiting further instructions. "Thank you, Mr. Simmons. I need the desk sergeant here now."

Picking up the phone, she punched out a number. The line was answered after the first ring.

"Director Sheldon."

"Director Sheldon, this is interim Director Laraby."

"Congratulations. I heard there was a bit of a shake-up over there. I'm glad to hear of your promotion and equally saddened by the departure of Director Bancroft. He will be missed."

"Thank you. And yes, he will be missed by all."

"What can I do for you Director Laraby?"

"You were informed of the problem that we are having involving our interests there in New Jersey?"

"Yes. Agent Mack kept me in the loop."

"It seems that we have a problem. Agent Mack has been killed and the agent that was with our interests is in the hospital and our interest is missing along with the associated baggage."

"This is not good. That interest was only just recovered. How can we help."

"I fear that this is an inside job. As long as the interest and the baggage are intact, the interest is secure. I would ask that you ground all departing fights in the tri-state area. Our time-line is that the person has a half hour head start on us. Our search is on-going."

"That's assuming that your traitor is going air borne. This is a big country and a half hour is an eternity, especially if this is one of your agents."

"The only way that the interest would be of any use is to get them out of the States."

"Director, let me be blunt. We came across some information as to the interest's origins and the impact it has on the Crown. What makes you believe that the interest will stay secure?"

"If the interest is compromised in anyway, then all bets are off."

She could hear him nodding. As much as she preferred a video conference, it was almost impossible to keep those secure.

"All right, Director Laraby. I'll get with Home Land Security and tell them that we have a with a suspected Al-Qaeda operative trying to get out of the country. Protocol will ground all outbound flights, commercial and private. We can buy you maybe six hours. That's about the best we can do."

"Thank you, Director. I'll keep you posted."

Laraby hung up the phone and sat back to consider the next move. She may have gotten her job through a devious method, but it didn't mean that she wasn't qualified for it.

Chapter 52

The killer sat in the back seat with a gun trained on T.J. Sara kept on glancing into the rear view mirror as the drove along the Turnpike. She had expected them to be heading toward an airport. Instead, they were heading south towards Pennsylvania. She remembered this route from the times she had been camping along the Delaware Water Gap.

T.J. was trying her best to look brave. Considering that the slight man holding the gun had held it against her head to force them into the car. T.J. had screamed hysterically when she saw Butler go down. There had been blood everywhere. Enough to traumatize a young child for years to come. Sara knew that if nothing else, she was going to kill him for that.

She was mentally taking stock of the situation. He had made her set the cruise control, so speeding to get the State Trooper's attention was out. She didn't have her phone. That was with Butler.

Sara had just seen him go by the window and figured that it would be the best time for her and the girls to get out, while they had him for coverage. Crawling out of the window silently, she then helped the girls through, one after the other. She had just hit the button for the door locks to open, when

149

the garbage can lid had lifted and a man popped out of the can.

She had tried to warn Butler, but it all happened so fast. The man hit Butler with the lid and blood had come pouring from his head then the can lid hit his wrist. Sara had almost thrown up when she heard the bone crunch.

Butler's gun had hit the grass by the drive. Lunging for it, she was met by the killer's foot stomping on her hand. The girls had been so scared that they had stood frozen to one spot, huddled together. The man leveled his gun in their direction while he bent down to get Butler's gun. Looking over at Butler's still form on the ground, he lifted the gun and pointed it at the agent's head. Sara, still on the ground, her hand pinned under his foot, lunged with all her might, hitting his knee and setting him off balance, staggering three or four steps. It was enough for Sara to scramble to her feet and start to run. A bullet grazed past her head and lodged into the side of the house. It had stopped her dead in her tracks, a few feet from the girls. She put her hands up and turned around. He then told them to get into the car and got in with them. Directing Sara from the back seat, she started the car and told her where to go. From then on it was one syllable directions that she followed without question. It was when he held the gun to T.J.'s head that Sara decided that this bastard must die.

Chapter 53

Butler woke up as he was being lifted into an ambulance. He tried sitting up but was restrained by one of the MI-6 agents. He remembered her as Agent Benson. She was short, but strong as an ox.

"Agent Butler. You have a broken wrist and a probable concussion. I stapled the wound on your head so it shouldn't bleed anymore. The most I can do for your wrist is to stabilize it for now. We can cast it back at the clinic. Other than a headache, how's the vision?"

"Good. No doubles or anything. How much of a lead does he have?"

"About a half hour, maybe less."

"Tim?"

She shook her head. "It was quick."

"Do we know who it is?"

Benson looked at him hard. "We were hoping you could tell us. All of our agents are accounted for. The Director had us do a visual accounting because she feels it's an inside job."

Butler looked up from his wrist "Did you say 'she'?"

"Yeah. Damnedest thing. Director Bancroft went out on a medical and Laraby was named interim director. Never saw that coming."

Shaking his head in disbelief, the shock momentarily short circuiting his brain "neither did I."

Chapter 54

Laraby knocked on the Prince's door for the second time in as many days. "enter" was the terse response she received.

She opened the door and went in, feeling like a lamb going into the lion's den. This was not a good way to start the job.

"Sir, our situation in New Jersey has gone from bad to worse. Agent Mack is dead, Agent Butler is being treated at our clinic and your daughter and her children are missing. The CIA has agreed to ground all flights leaving the states for 6 hours."

The Prince stood up, his face drained of color then it bloomed bright red. "ARE YOU BLOODY SERIOUS?! HOW THE HELL DID THIS HAPPEN?!"

The Director was proud of herself that she hadn't flinched.

"Sir. We have reason to believe that this is an inside job. All of our agents are accounted for, now we are working on staff. So far we have three unaccounted for and we are tracking them down."

He sat back and looked at Laraby, struggling to get his emotions under control. " You believe this why..."

"Your Highness. Agent Mack was on the way to Sara's house when he was killed. He was taken by surprise in his car. He had spoken to Agent Butler who told him to meet him at Sara's, but he didn't elaborate. Butler hasn't regained consciousness as of yet. But Agent Mack had received a communique that confirmed that your oldest son is behind the hit on the line. Sir, we have all of the evidence we need to not only charge him but also to convict him of high treason."

"All right. Bring him in to me."

Laraby shook her head. "Sir. I would suggest we hold off on that for a time. Sara and the children were taken as a bargaining chip. If the Prince knows that the game is up, he has no reason to keep them alive nor help in their recovery. I would suggest that we let things go on as they are for a time. The CIA has grounded things for 6 hours. Let's use that as best as we can to locate your daughter."

The Prince thought about it for a minute. He played out every possible scenario imaginable. It all came to the same conclusion. Sara and his grandchildren dead. He nodded. "I assume that my son is still ignorant that he is a suspect?"

"Yes Sir. He is at the safe house under guard. He has been told that there is a credible threat to the line and for his own protection he is being kept hidden and as planned all of the successors are being hidden separately from each other."

"Good. This will make things easier. You do know what has to be done when this is all over?"

Laraby only knew too well. She had been posing as a skiing tourist the last time a threat had to be neutralized. Acts of treason were not tolerated.

Chapter 55

─────────

Sara looked over at Cassidy. The girl was flushed and had a slight sweat sheen on her upper lip. She tapped her pocket very slightly. Puzzled, Sara thought for a second. Her phone! Cassidy had her phone with her.

Since it hadn't rung in a while, it was probably shut off. But if she turned it on, the phone's start up music would come on, giving them away. She gave a small nod to Cassidy and tucked a finger on the steering wheel. Then another. As Sara tucked the third finger she hit the button on the steering wheel that controlled the volume on the radio. It was loud enough that it momentarily shocked everyone in the car. Three things happened in that instant. The killer grabbed Sara by her hair and jabbed the gun into her temple causing the car to swerve, T.J. screamed and started to cry and Cassidy was able to turn her phone on, activating the GPS signal chip inside.

Chapter 56

Butler was waiting for the cast to finish setting. He had been x-rayed back at the Brownstone in the basement clinic. On more than one occasion, surgery had been done in that room. The x-ray revealed that he had a slight concussion, his wrist was broken in two places and that he was definitely going to need to take a few days off.

Two hours had passed since Sara and the girls had been taken. Her car's GPS had been disabled and they personal locaters were not responding. Sara's phone was with him and the phones that the girl's had were wither turned off or disabled.

Agent Riggins sat down next to Butler, in what had been Tim's desk.

Butler looked over at her "I knew Tim for the better part of fifteen years. It's hard to believe that he's gone." "I know what you mean. He chose me for this assignment. Somehow I feel as if I let him down."

Shaking his head, Butler touched her arm with his good hand. "Tim knew what he was doing. He trusted that everyone here was on the same team. Speaking of which, anything on the missing three?"

Riggins shook her head. "It's as if they fell off the face of the earth. All three logged off of the computers at the same time yesterday afternoon when their shift ended. They were last seen together at the pub down the street. The three of them got into a cab together and that is the last we heard of them. We checked with the cab company. The drivers remembers letting them off at the corner of 42nd and Broadway. The street camera has them going into an apartment a few blocks away. None of the looked as if they were being forced or under any kind of duress. They never came out, least not where a camera would see them. It's a dead end. We've come to the conclusion that one or all three of them are in on this."

"I agree. So, let me see the files on all three."

Chapter 57

"You stupid bitch! Turn that fucking radio down!"

He had Sara by a handful of hair and was pulling her head back. She pushed the button and silenced the radio. He kept a hold of her hair while she struggled to keep the car from swerving. "I'm sorry! I'm sorry! I hit the button by accident. It's a habit. I didn't mean to do it." Sara as careful to keep her voice scared.

She was reasonably sure that he wouldn't shoot her while the car was in motion. If he was going to kill them, he would have done so at the house. He was obviously going to great pains to keep them alive, but Sara didn't know for how long and for what purpose. Alive didn't mean unharmed.

"Unless you want a bullet in one of your brats, I would suggest that you be a little more careful." he hissed into her ear. He abruptly released her head but kept the gun at her temple.

"yes, I will. I am sorry." The silence in the car was deafening.

T.J. was softly sobbing into her stuffed animal book bag. Sara looked back at her in the rear view, but all she could see was the man's head. She looked into his blue eyes and was immediately shocked at how crystal blue they were. He looked back and smiled.

"Yes. People are often surprised at how blue they are. You'd be surprised how much trouble they get me into. Both a blessing and a curse. I'm told that my grandfather had the same problem."

He sat back and looked at the back of Cassidy's head then back over at T.J. Keeping he gun trained on the younger child, he smiled down at her stuffed animal. "Amazing the things that parent's will buy for their kids, eh?"

Looking at the road ahead of them, Sara wondered where they were going. As if he were reading her mind "Take this exit, to the right."

"Mind telling us where we are going?"

"We are going to meet some friends of mine. They want to introduce themselves to you and your girls. I promised that I would help make the introductions."

"And what are you going to get out of it?"

"Would you believe that I am doing this out of the kindness of my heart?"

Sara snorted "Yeah, right. Uhm, I don't think so."

"Quite right. Actually, I am getting a sort of finders fee, if you will. I deliver the three of you and I get six million dollars. Two million each is the going rate for a bastard Royal."

Chapter 58

Butler looked at the three files in front of him. Hardy, Marvis and Canon. All three were MI-6 trained computer techs. None of them had ever been in the field and none of them had ever been anything but computer geniuses. They had all gone through the training but it had been more cursory than actual. All three were qualified with small arms. None were married or had any significant attachments.

This wasn't going to work. He handed one to Riggins and one to another agent, Thompson. "Look. We don't know if these guys are working together or apart. Let's act like cops and work each one of these guys up as if they are all suspects. Two hours are down. I agree with the Director. Once this guy can, he's going airborne. 30 minutes and we meet back here and see what we've put together."

Just then one of the techs jumped up with a whoop of excitement. "One of the kid's phone just turned on. The GPS has them on the Pennsylvania Turnpike."

Butler got up and taking Riggin's folder from her, threw all three of them at Thompson. "Work them up. Call us when you know who is what. you've got thirty minutes. Tell us who and what we are dealing with. Let's go." He said over his shoulder to Riggins. She didn't even try to argue with him. Something in his stance told her it would be useless.

Chapter 59

Sara looked at the GPS on the dashboard. They were definitely heading to the Water Gap. The problem was that this time of year, there was nothing out there except miles and miles of forests, camp ground and hunting lodges. A person could get lost out there and die. Or keep someone captive indefinitely. This was not good. All she could hope was that someone from MI-6 was paying attention to the cell phones. She sent up a silent prayer.

The killer had settled back, but still had the gun trained on T.J. Occasionally he would check the speedometer over Sara's shoulder, a subtle reminder for her not to speed.

"Take this exit." He ordered. They were heading to Dingman's Ferry. Barry had taken the kids there many summers for camping trips. Lots and lots of forest. it was prime hunting area. And since they were in between seasons, it would surely be deserted. Sara's heart almost sank. All she could hope was that she could make someone notice them.

As she made plans and tried to figure escapes routes in her head, a faint jingling came from Cassidy's pocket. For an instant, no one breathed. Then everything went into slow motion. Sara saw the killer turn the gun to Cassidy, She jerked the wheel hard to the left and T.J. began to give a blood curdling scream. Then the tires screamed in protest before the entire jeep rolled over. And as it rolled down the embankment, a shot rang out. There was blood everywhere.

Chapter 60

Butler was watching the GPS signal on his computer. They had made good time and were within an hour of their location. Their target was continuing south.

A program running probable destinations continued to plot their possible destinations. Then the signal stopped moving. It was still active, but it had stopped moving. Butler blew up the location from the satellite feed. Since they had been able to "hitchhike" on a satellite that was currently over them, they feed was real time. As he zoomed in, he could see Sara's jeep laying on it's roof on the side of the road. Far enough off the road so as not to attract attention, but clear enough to see if you were looking for it.

"Shit. Riggins, get the locals on the phone, let them know that we have a hostage-kidnapping situation of a British citizen. They are to proceed with caution. There could be as many as three abductors, they are armed and considered dangerous. Also inform them that there are two children, U.S. citizens, involved. Answer all of the questions that you can, just make sure they get someone in the forest and an ambulance out to the car." Butler felt his stomach go into a panic. Much the same way when Katey failed to come up from the snow avalanche that had engulfed them while they had been on holiday. He knew, before the search had even begun that his beautiful wife was gone. But this was different. Sara was alive. She was in grave danger, but she was alive.

Chapter 61

Sara was the first to recover, but the killer was two beats behind her. He kicked the door open and staggered out, standing up slowly. Sara looked over to Cassidy. There was blood coming from her shoulder. She was out cold. Sara could see that she was breathing and the blood was seeping, not pulsing out. It wasn't arterial, but it was still a bullet in her baby. T.J.'s soft voice came from the back. "Mommy, is Cassidy dead?"

Sara shook her head and tried to steady her voice. "No honey, but this is bad."

T.J. began to wail. The killer pulled the door open and pointed it at Sara. "Get out now or I'll finish her off."

It struck her as almost comedic. She was hanging upside down and there was blood everywhere and T.J.'s hysterical wailing wasn't making it any better. The little girl had already released the seatbelt and had one arm around her mother's head, stuffed animal bag clutched in a death grip . Sara reached to release her own seat belt with one hand and supported herself on the roof of the car to control her fall. She slithered out from the car and pulled T.J. out with her. The killer never took his gun from her. He had the other gun trained on T.J. Sara went over to the other side to get Cassidy out.

He motioned her away from the car. "No. Leave her. Someone is bound to see the car. There is that little matter of the cell phone so I'm sure the team is hot on our trail. She won't be alone too long. Now let's go, or do you want the little one to join her sister over there?"

Sara felt panic and desperation rising in her chest. "At least let me pull her out of there. If the car catches fire, she won't stand a chance. Please. Have mercy. She is just a little girl."

He must have seen the panic begin in her eyes. He knew that a panicked woman or a distraught mother were unpredictable at best.

"Fine, pull her out and get me her phone." Sara almost flew to open the door. She gently released the belt and cushioned Cassidy's fall. Dragging her to an area clear of the car, she then ripped open the shirt and did her best to make a pressure dressing. Cassidy moaned lightly and her eyes fluttered open. Sara slightly shook her head and the girl became silent. They both knew that one of them had to get out of this to get help.

Looking up at the killer, Sara looked him in the eyes to keep him from looking at Cassidy too hard. "She's still unconscious. We shouldn't move her."

He nodded "I agree. We won't move her. She would only slow us down. Now throw her phone over here. That's a good lass. Just on the off chance that they haven't got a fix on us."

He smashed the phone and took out the battery. He threw the phone as far as he could then walked over to where Sara was kneeling next to Cassidy. Both mother and daughter were saying a silent prayer that he bought the ruse. He brought the gun to point it at the girl. Sara jumped up and stood in front of him.

"You'll have to shoot me first. And somehow I don't think your finders fee is for dead bodies."

He considered for a second then pulled the gun back to her. "You're right, of course and while this whole thing has cost me two mill, at least I still have you and the little one. Leave her and let's go, or the crier here will get real quiet."

Sara let out a sigh of relief. At least one of her babies was going to make it out of this alive. She knew in her heart that Butler was coming. It was that belief that gave her the strength to give her daughter's hand one last squeeze then stand up and leave.

Chapter 62

R iggins' phone rang. She answered it then handed it to Butler. "Yeah. Thompson,slow down. Now try it again, we are near some mountains."

"Two bodies washed up at the Island Beach State park this morning. I'm still waiting for i.d. but it could be two of our lads. Butler, I've checked the financials and one of our boys has a bad gambling problem. We're talking knee breakers and Crown secrets kind of gambling."

"Which one?"

"Mavin. He's white, five foot six and a hundred eighty five pounds. Blond hair, blue eyes and he fancies himself the ladies man. He is also a computer genius to end all computer geeks. I'm sure that this is our guy. The other thing that clinches it for me is that his history says he spent much of his youth out in this area with his grandparents during summers and holidays. He was a real boy scout. Kind of a Davey Crockett."

"If that is what your gut and your proof is telling you, run with it. Send his picture to every agency from here to Canada. If this guy knows the area, he is really going to be hard to find. Also, get over to Sara's mother's house, put her on a chopper to the Pocono Medical Center. Just tell her that there has been an accident and that one of her granddaughters is there, nothing more than that for now. Out."

Butler went back to watching the screen. Problem was that the images were sent after a minute had passed, and with each passing minute, the ache in his belly was getting worse.

Each feed came as a frame, like a slow motion slide show. The next picture showed first Mavin out of the overturned car. Then him pointing a gun into the car. Sara getting out with one of the children. Sara bent over a small form and another child standing next to Mavin with a gun pointing at her small head. The next frame was them walking away, leaving a child laying next to the car. Butler's blood ran cold. Mavin would never make it to trial. The same thought went through every person in the car.

Chapter 62

Agent Thompson knocked on the ornately carved wood door. It was almost immediately opened by an attractive older woman. Sara looked surprisingly like her mother, with the exception of the salt and pepper hair, they could have been sisters.

Maria was stressed beyond her last nerve. First Sara calling her and telling her that they were leaving immediately, then all of the black SUVs and an ambulance at her daughter's house had only made it worse. Nobody was telling her anything. When she had opened the door to the stranger dressed in Black BDUs, she wasn't in a friendly state of mind. "Can I help you?"

He handed her his i.d. for her to inspect. "Ma'am. I am Agent Thompson. Team Leader Riggins has sent me to get you and put you on a helicopter to Stroudsburg, Pennsylvania. There has been an accident and your granddaughter was taken to that facility."

"Oh my God! Which one?! What about my daughter?!" the door was pulled open further and an entire crowd stared at the agent.

Amanda stepped froward. "What the hell are you talking about?!"

Thompson was beginning to fell threatened. Guns he could handle. Dominate and angry women made him twitch. It also put some steel into his tone.

"Mrs. Inverso, would you also come with us. I have a feeling before all of this is over, your assistance will be needed. I will explain further on the way."

Barry stepped forward as if to come also. Thompson held up his hand. "Mr. Cohen, it would be better if you followed in a car. The trip is a few hours...."

"I know where it is. We used to go camping up there. We still ski up there."

"very good, sir. Then we will meet you at the Pocono Medical Center. Now, ladies, if you could, we must hurry."

Chapter 63

Sara had to trust the feeling that Butler was coming and would rescue her baby.

She helped T.J. as much as she could, but neither was dressed for this. Sara had taken enough time to change into jeans and a t-shirt, as had the girls, but only the girls had changed into sneakers. She was in flats. Good for walking on pavement, not so much for the woods. Several times she had to stop to take things out of them. That just pissed off their captor even more.

She saw a log and sat down. Mavin pointed the gun at her. "I didn't say stop. Get up and get moving or I'll have to persuade you another way."

She looked him dead in the eyes and suddenly she was tired of being pushed around. First her ex-husband, then the trial and now this. It was enough

She exhaled deeply, resolutely. "Look. It's like this. The only thing keeping me from killing you is my daughter, the one you keep putting a gun to. Now, if you kill her or wound her, you have taken away your only bargaining chip. So, I will keep walking as soon as I am ready. Since we are heading out of the woods and presumably to some meeting place where you have agreed to deliver us, there is no hurry. You have patted us both down and know that we do not have any kind of weapons or electronic devices with us. That being the case, we have no way of contacting anyone with our location. Also, we have no way of knowing our way out of this God forsaken forest. You *obviously* know where you are going. We are going to rest a minute, then we will go. Got it?"

Mavin stared at her, a look of pure incredulous on his face Then his humor returned. "fair enough. Even if you did escape, I would still be able to find you. My grandparents live up in these woods. We spent many summers tracking and hunting in these woods."

"Well, isn't that just peachy for you. I don't suppose you have anything with you to eat or drink?"

"No, your highness." he sneered through his smile. "But the cabin we are going to is not too far from here. It is fully stocked and has all of the amenities to make you comfortable. Now, if you and T.J. have had enough of a rest, I would like to get going. Even with a head start, we are going to have a tough time keeping ahead of the Team. Then we will probably have the locals to deal with."

Getting up, her mind went into overdrive. She had a pretty good idea where they were. The problem came back to her that even if she and T.J. did escape, he had a gun and some reasonable tracking skills. She was watching how he blurred their tracks as the walked and was careful to check the brush for snagged clothing or broken branches. He was behind them, so catching him by surprise was going to be tough.

As they walked, Sara noticed that this was probably a hunting path. Here and there she would see deer blinds up in the trees. Hunters would make small platforms in the trees about six to eight feet off the ground. This would allow them to wait for a deer to come out and not detect the hunter too easily. It also gave the hunter a better shot. And with hunters, you had coffee and other beverages. Cups were scattered about, giving Sara an idea.

"Excuse me, Since I don't know your name, is it much further, because I have to pee so badly that it is getting difficult to walk,"

As if on cue, T.J. chimed in with "Me, too."

Mavin let out a sigh of exasperation. "Fine. Go behind the tree right there. I imagine that you both can't pee in front of a man. One at a time. And you little girl, try anything and I will shoot your Mum and leave you here for the bears to eat."

Fear flashed over T.J.'s face for a moment. Then her mother's spirit showed itself. "I'm not afraid of you. My grandpa is coming and he's bringing Butler with him."

Amusement flashed across his face. "Little girl, I am not afraid of your grandfather and I have made sure that even if Agent Butler comes after me, he won't be in any shape to do anything about it. Now go over there and pee before I make you piss yourself."

Sara was surprised. She knew that the girls had been aware of Butler's outburst, but she didn't think that they would take it to heart. She prayed that the little girl was right and wasn't betrayed by her own innocence.

Chapter 64

It seemed an eternity watching the monitor from the satellite feed until the cop car got to the overturned vehicle and then an ambulance pulled up. Everyone let out a sigh of relief when the ambulance was followed by a paramedic rig and the little girl was loaded into it. While the detail was hard to make out, everyone knew that they don't load a dead body into a paramedic rig. Monitoring the police band, they were able to know that is was Cassidy that was out of the kidnapper's hands and on the way to the hospital. It eased Butler's mind to some degree, but just strengthened his reasons for killing Mavin.

Riggins called up the local police and the State troopers for an update. They confirmed what they had assumed. The local sheriff informed them that Cassidy had given them a good description of the kidnapper as well as the direction they were heading. Tracking dogs were being ordered in and that they would be deployed in under a half hour.

Thompson had the foresight to have Maria call the hospital to let them know that she was a named guardian and was en route to the hospital. She also gave verbal permission for them to treat, stopping at permission for surgery since Cassidy was stable and the bullet was securely lodged in her shoulder.

Riggins thought it was an oxymoron, "a bullet lodged securely in a child's shoulder". Thompson told her that they would be at the hospital in less than a half hour. He would up date her as soon as there was anything else to report.

Butler looked at his watch. three hours and counting. He pulled up a map on his computer. There was a commuter airport about thirty miles from where Cassidy was found. There were also various cabins strewn about. The woods were dense and being nearly summer, the trees were full and providing lots of cover. This was not going to be easy. Conversation inside the SUV was at a standstill. Everyone was playing out scenario after scenario to see the best play.

Looking over Butler's shoulder, Riggins held out her hand. "B...let me see your unit for a minute." He handed it to her. She hit a few strokes on the key pad.

Letting out a "whoop" she handed it back. "I just enabled the infrared scan from the satellite link. It's looking into heat signatures. The only problem is that you have to get closer to distinguish two legged animals from four legged ones. But you can see here, it isn't that much of a target rich environment." She pulled out her phone and rang up the sheriff's phone. "Sheriff Hoagland, this is agent Riggins again. About 30 meters from where the Cohen girl was found we can see a heat signature. Yeah, our computer guys are top notch. Unfortunately, we can't get more than that, but it is a good place to start. Yes, Sir, I will keep you updated. No, unfortunately I can't link you up. Our systems being so different and all. Yes sir, I'll do that. Riggins out." She pushed the button to disconnect the call.

She smiled at Butler's raised eyebrow. "It's always a good idea to make nice with the locals. You never know when they will come in handy."

"Did he say anything else?"

"Nothing we didn't already know. They are deploying dogs from an area not on our scope" She took the computer back again and scrolled the screen until they were able to make out the heat signatures that were bunched together and moving fast. "See here, that would be the sheriff's people with their hounds. I've seen these animals at work. They know their business."

Chapter 65

Sara watched as T.J. made her way to a tree about twenty feet away. "Mommy, I can't pee without getting my shoes wet." The little girl's voice wavered again, as if she were on the verge of tears. Looking over at Mavin "Come on. Let me help her. She has never peed in anything but a toilet."

Rolling his eyes at her "City girls. Fine go help her, but the first thing that looks out of place, I'll put a bullet in her leg."

Sara muffled a snort as she walked over to the struggling little girl. As she bent over help her squat, she moved a plastic cup under T.J. to catch the falling liquid. After she helped her get her pants back up, Sara leaned against the tree and aimed for the cup. She gave herself a mental smile. A man couldn't have done better. A she pulled up her pants, she stooped down to make it look like she was emptying her shoe. On her way back up, she palmed the cup.

Mavin came over to them and motioned with the gun. "If you ladies are done with bodily functions, can we go now? It will soon be dark and it gets a lot tougher walking then."

Sara looked around and picked a direction. Then she spun, pushed T.J. to the ground and threw the warm liquid into Mavin's eyes. While the man howled in shock and pain, she grabbed T.J.'s hand and was off and running, aiming for a clump of trees about twenty feet in front of her. She heard Mavin yell to stop. She heard the gun fire and almost instantly felt the bullet lodge into a tree a couple of feet from her. She dragged T.J. and did her best to serpentine. They made it to the trees. she picked her next direction and went that way. She cringed when another bullet hit a tree not far from where they were. Another bullet and another. It was hard to hit a moving target, even harder to hit two. T.J. fell and was promptly drug to her feet as they kept running. Sara veered to the left then to the right. As they got deeper into the forest, the trees were getting further apart. It was hard to tell if they were going in a straight line or in circles. The bullets stopped whizzing past them. Was he out? Was he waiting for her to run into him?.

She stood still for a second and listened. For a moment all she hear was her's and T.J.'s heavy breathing. Looking down into the little girl's face, Sara held up a finger to her lips and shook her head. Then she heard the brush breaking under a foot. It was heading away from her. She slowly slid down to the ground at the base of the tree. And far off in the distance was the sound of a hound dog. She would know that howling anywhere. If a hound dog was out there, then rescue was on it's way. And if she heard it, then the killer had heard it too. And then right next to her, she felt his breath in her ear. "Gotcha"

Chapter 66

They were ten minutes away from the scene, but Butler felt like it was fifty years. He checked the speedometer. Covington was doing an even hundred. Butler almost told him to push it faster, but in this big beast, it was had to maintain speed and control, so he let him be. Didn't mean that he wasn't thinking it.

Riggins looked over at him. "She's going to be alright, you know. If he hadn't killed her in the first few minutes, then he is waiting for a payoff and not too many people will pay for dead body."

Nodding "I know you're right. Doesn't make me worry any less. Pull up that link again. How long before we can get satellite feed again?"

She pulled up the link then looked at her watch. "It won't be in position again for another half hour. We could probably patch in to another cell phone one, but we won't have infrared reads, just real time photos."

"Damn , we'll be there by then."

Riggins turned around to face him better. "Did I mention that in this area, despite what you see on the telly, these Yanks seem to know their stuff when it comes to law enforcement. Granted, there are very few good enough to make the Team, but you have to believe that they can handle things until we get there.

She laid a hand on his cast to get his attention. "Butler, you need to put your emotions in check. I let you come along because I know that Tim said you were the best. There may be some who think that an emotional attachment can help when it comes to a rescue operation like this- I am not one of them. If I think for an instant that you are letting your heart get in the way of this rescue, I will cuff you to the bumper. Do I make myself clear?"

Sucking in his lower lip and looking down, he nodded. She was right. He had to get his emotions in check and be the professional that he was trained to be. Then after Sara was rescued, He'd kill the bastard.

Chapter 67

"That was very foolish of you" Mavin hissed into her ear. And without even blinking, he shot Sara in the foot.

She rolled on the ground screaming. The pain was so intense, she almost fainted. Hearing T.J. scream in horror and feeling the little girl's small body falling on her made Sara hang on. But she didn't have time to get a handle on the pain before he drug her up by her hair.

"Now, I told you that I would shoot the brat, but it occurred to me that you were right. So now you can't run, but you can still walk. And unfortunately for my colleagues, there are dogs after us. The drop off site is less than thirty meters that way. And when I drop you I can leave. Now get up or I will shoot your arm out. Like you pointed out they want you alive, but I don't remember anyone saying anything about uninjured. Now move!"

It took everything in her not to scream in pain. She could feel her shoe filling up with blood, every step forcing out more.She looked down and could see a bloody footprint leaving a gory trail behind them. So much for him trying to hide their location.

As they went further, the trees began to clear a bit, the brush becoming thinner. She could see the top of a blue SUV, the luggage rack was glinting in the light. Sara began to feel lightheaded, the edges of her sight becoming blurry. When she swayed a bit, T.J. put her small arm around her mother's waist to help support her.

They were in line of sight to a small hunting cabin. Sara could see deer antlers adorning the outside and horse shoes over the door frame, put there for luck. As they got closer, the door of the cabin opened and two burly men came running over to them. One of them picked her up and the other picked up T.J. They were both carried to the SUV and pushed in. The one that had been carrying Sara shut the door and turned to face Mavin. Without a word, he shot him in the face.

"I told him I wanted you and your daughters unharmed." Sara looked to the front seat and looked into the palest blue eyes that she had ever seen. And in that instant, she truly knew fear.

Chapter 68

Maria and Amanda got off the helicopter as fast as they could. They were met by the e.r. nurse who was escorting them from the roof. Nearly running down the corridor, Thompson brought up the rear to make sure that there were no more surprises.

A local cop had been placed on each entrance to the hospital and a state trooper had been placed in the e.r. outside of Cassidy's room.

No one knew exactly why all of the protection was necessary, but the rumors had her placed as a witness, a senator's child to some kind of pop star. She had been given a pain killer so she was out of it when her aunt and grandmother came in. The doctor was on their heels when they were allowed in by the trooper. Thompson stayed with the family on the inside of the room. It was with great shame to the Team that this had happened. And though he knew there was no going back to undo the damage, he was in a position to prevent any further tragedies- and he would die trying.

Cassidy opened her eyes and held out her good hand to reach for Maria. As the doctor droned on about the need for immediate surgery. Amanda stepped in and listened to the doctor and signed the forms for anesthesia and surgery.

Maria lovingly brushed Cassidy's hair from the child's face as tears streaked down her own cheeks. There was blood all over her precious grandbaby. Cassidy was covered with a sheet, but was left nude for the surgery. What was visible above the sheet was streaked with blood. Her hair was matted with it, since the shoulder wound had bled profusely while she had been held upside down in the overturned car. Maria looked up at Thompson "I thought you guys were supposed to prevent this from happening."

"Ma'am, one agent is dead and another has a concussion and a broken wrist trying to prevent this. Unfortunately, it was an inside job. We know who the traitor is and we are hunting him down even as we speak."

Cassidy looked up at her grandmother. "Gamma," she said groggily "It's not his fault. The man came out of the garbage can. He smashed Butler with the lid and I think he hit him in the arm. Mom yelled at him and the guy was going to shoot Butler while he was on the ground. He pointed the gun at me and T.J. and we all got into the car." Her voice was very tired, but she knew she had to tell them what had happened. She had to make sure that her Grandmother knew that it wasn't the agents fault.

Forcing her eyes to remain open, she took a breath "He made Momma drive to the place by where we used to go camping. While were driving, I turned on my phone. The man was going to shoot me and Mom jerked the car hard one way and the car rolled over. That's when I got shot. I heard the gun and I felt the bullet hit me and then everything was upside down. Mom pulled me out. I pretended to by knocked out and he forced Mom to walk away from me. He told her that if she didn't leave, he would shoot T.J. Mom had to...." she fell asleep mid-sentence.

Maria looked up at the monitors to make sure that she still had a pulse and was breathing. The doctor felt her neck for a pulse and nodded. "She going to be all right, Mrs. Cohen. I'm surprised she even woke up. The sedative was strong enough to put out an adult. I need to get her into surgery. While we aren't afraid of the bullet moving from it's position it isn't doing her any good in there."

Maria nodded and held the girl's hand until the nurses and orderlies came to wheel Cassidy from the room. As they all squeezed into the elevator, the trooper was relieved to go on break and meet them on the surgical floor. He would be placed on post outside of the operating room while Thompson would be in the the o.r. itself.

The surgeon had done a residency in D.C. He knew that when a high level security presence was in the area, you didn't ask who it was, you just went along with the extra security measures. And while he didn't know who Cassidy Peterson was, she must be pretty important to warrant all of this. He watched form the window of the scrub room as the armed British agent put on scrubs over his clothes, leaving the bottom edge of the shirt tucked behind his gun to leave it free to pull out rapidly, should it be necessary.

The surgeon sent up a silent prayer that it wouldn't be necessary then held up his hands for the scrub nurse to hand him a towel. "Show time" he thought and went into the operating room.

Chapter 69

Sara watched, horrified at what she had just seen. Fortunately, T.J. had been so preoccupied with the giant of a man that had gently placed her in the vehicle, that she hadn't seen their abductor fall to the ground. Now the little girl was so bugged eyed looking at the man in the front seat. She didn't see the two giants push the body onto a ditch along side the driveway of the cabin.

The older man looked out of the window and nodded. He then opened the door and signaled for one of the men to help Sara and T.J. from the car. It was an odd looking group that headed back to the cabin. As Sara was carried effortlessly though the door she wondered what the hell was going to happen next and how she could get T.J. out of it safely.

As they went into the dark cabin, the older man turned on lights to illuminate the small room. Sara was placed on a chair next to the small table. She let out a hiss when her foot scraped the ground.

The blue-eyed man turned to the giant, concern plainly written on his face.

"Get the first aid kit and let's get her foot taken care of, at least as best as we can."

One of the giants left the room and went back outside. Sara presumed that it was where the first aid kit was. T.J. also sat at the table. She got up and stood behind her mother, patting her shoulder to reassure her as the best she could. Sara felt the blood pooled in her shoe. Since it was cooled a bit, Sara was partially relieved that the bleeding had slowed down.

Standing in front of her, the older man pulled over another chair to sit next to her. "I do apologize for all of this, Ms. Cohen. When I had hired Mavin- your abductor, to get you, he had been under strict instructions that neither you nor your children were to be harmed in any way, other than the obvious fear that is associated with being abducted."

Sara didn't know what to think. One part of her was scared to death for T.J. and herself. Another part was enraged, that this was the brains behind her abduction and her child being shot. Then there was the part that was cheering, because Mavin (so that was his name) was dead. And who the hell was this guy?

Holding out a hand to her "Let me introduce myself. I am James Bancroft, as of late, the former Director of MI-6."

Chapter 70

Butler's phone vibrated. They were taking the last exit to the car crash site, the last known location for Sara and T.J. He looked down at it. The text read "they are fine call me james". What the hell? he thought .

Pulling out his phone, Butler dialed the number.

Riggins was talking to the local sheriff. They were on the trail and felt that they were getting close.

On the second ring, the lines connected. "James? Butler. What the hell is going on?"

A light chuckle on the other end, a voice that Butler had known for years, should have been reassuring, but at that moment, it made his blood run cold.

"Butler, my old friend. I have been listening and watching the reports. I am glad that you are going to be all right. I have Ms. Cohen and her daughter with me. Have the dogs and locals stay outside of the cabin and come in when you get here. I will explain everything then."

The line went silent. Butler looked up at Riggins. She was still on the phone getting a blow by blow report from the sheriff's officer on the scene. "They have a blood trail and are following it to a hunting cabin."

"Tell them once they get there to post outside. No one goes in or comes out until I get there."

Looking puzzled, Riggings relayed the message then closed her phone. "Care to let a girl in on what's going on?"

He shrugged "I'm not sure. I just received instructions that they are safe and to come to the cabin when we get there."

Chapter 71

One of the agents, at least Sara presumed they were agents, gently took Sara's shoe off. T.J. had refused to leave her mother's side, but at the sight of the blood had been persuaded to sit on the opposite side of the table. T.J. could see her mother, but not the activity going on below table level.

"I am very sorry that you were shot." Jame explained "Cassidy is in surgery even as we speak. Your mother and your sister, Amanda were flown out to Stroudsburg to be with her. She has a bullet wound to the shoulder, which you already knew. Other than that, she is expected to make a full recovery. She was only alone out there for a few minutes. If you had been able to delay Mavin for five minutes, the local trooper would have intercepted you."

The agent on the floor was soaking her foot in a bowl of cool water. The water cleaned out the wound but also started the bleeding again. It wasn't flowing with blood, but it was making things nasty. As gently as he could, he applied a pressure dressing, drawing fresh hisses of pain from Sara.

"Be careful there Stewart. It looks as if the bullet went all the way through, but it will need sutures. The hospital will take care of that shortly."

Sara looked back to him, "How do you know all of this?"

"Which part? The abduction or the aftermath?"

"All of it" she said slowly, not exactly sure that they were indeed two different parts.

"I'll try to make this quick. Butler is on his way here and I do need to make a quick get away, as it were. Since you were a small infant, I have been telling your father- the Prince, not Mr. Cohen- that you were at risk out in the open like this.. That it wouldn't take much, just the abduction and ransom of a Royal, to topple the Crown. He didn't believe me. Matter of fact, it was that very thing-my questioning his decisions, that helped my deputy director to steal my job. So, I put into play your abduction. And in one move, I was able to show that my theory was correct."

"What about the Prince's son and his girlfriend?" Sara was trying to distract herself from the wrapping and pain that her foot was in.

"Here, Stewart" James handed him a bottle of pills. "Give her two of those."

"Are these safe, or are you finishing up what Mavin started?" She was dubiously looking at the pills that the agent handed her.

"Oh, no my dear" he chuckled. It wasn't an ominous chuckle and Sara thought, another time and other circumstances, she could like this man. He reminded her of James Coburn, in a British kind of way. "Those are some mild pain killers. I don't want t give you any aspirin or thing like that. Since you will have some work on that foot, we don't want to make you bleed any more than you have to. They won't incapacitate you or anything else, but they will take the edge off. "

He adjusted himself to face her more fully."No. You dead was not one of the goals for this test. Exposing my country's weaknesses was. The younger Prince's involvement was and is very real."

"He orchestrated the murder of the line of succession, his own relatives. That was his plan. the hard part was to find a group that would do it. I provided that group. Sort of a sting operation. And while I was the lowest bidder. I wasn't the only one to try to get the contract. If I hadn't been successful, you and your children would have been dead for sure. Mavin thought he was working for a Muslim terrorist who paid him six million to abduct the three of you. I suppose that is why he went to such an elaborate extent to carry out the task. He was up to his neck in debt and was desperate."

"Was my e-husband art of this plan?"

Shaking his head "No. That was just one of those opportunities that couldn't be ignored. You had been placed so off the radar and on the back burner, that your ex-husband wasn't even thought of as a threat. But when you disappeared, and the hit was already being shopped around, it just seemed logical to put my plan into motion. If it makes you feel more secure, Mr. Peterson has contracted a rare form of stomach cancer." He pointedly looked over at T.J., who hadn't taken her eyes off of him since he started to speak. "He isn't likely to make a recovery."

Looking down, she let this digest. She looked over at T.J. and could tell that she hadn't totally absorbed the meaning behind the statement. Well, death was a reality and Sara couldn't shield her kids from everything. Their father dying, while indirectly was her fault, was his own making. One less thing for Sara to worry about.

"Well Mr. Bancroft. I don't know whether to thank you or be horrified."

He raised an eyebrow "Thank you, works.. Especially since I know what he did."

T.J. found her voice "My Daddy didn't do anything. He left us years ago because he couldn't handle the responsibility of a family."

James gave a sideways look at Sara before he made eye contact with T.J. Not a man to be unnecessarily cruel, he wasn't going to let this child live with this lie in her head.

"I am sorry to be the one to tell you this, Ms. Peterson. But your father kidnapped your mother earlier this week. And despite your mother trying to protect you from some awful truths, your father had a mental breakdown. He is currently in a hospital where he can't hurt you, your sister or your mother."

The girl was not going to give up on her father so quickly. She had heard lots of whispering where he was concerned and while part of her had always dreamed of the long lost father returning to his family, she wasn't a fool. She watched t.v., read books. She knew that something was wrong with him. She wasn't prepared to let go of the fantasy, some glimmer of hope remained that her Daddy was the knight in shining armor she always dreamed of when she was sent to her room or her sister was picking on her. It was the same fantasy that all little girls had when their father was out of the picture.

James knew this. He also knew that it was destructive, especially when you had a father willing to sell you to pay debts, or kidnap your mother, rape her and hold her hostage in the name of God. A man with those kinds of mental problems did not deserve to live, much less, did not deserve a family as good as this one.

He pulled his chair around so that now he was looking T.J, directly in the eyes.

"Miss Peterson, understand me when tell you that you are better off without him. It may sound terrible when I say it, but this is the truth. You are a wonderful person. You are a good daughter to your mother and a wonderful granddaughter to your grandparents."

"Some people don't know when they have the best in their lives. Your father is one of those people. When he walked away from you and your sister, he left the best thing in the world-a family that loved him. And whereas some people come to their senses and change for the better, your father didn't. He did change, became different, but not a good kind of different. He became worse. You are better off without him. And that isn't my opinion, it is a fact. When a man can kidnap his children's mother and threaten her, he doesn't love her or those children. That is not love. That is being selfish. I should know. My father was that kind of person. He beat me and my sister, killed our mother and still said he loved us. I did not want to see that happen to you or Cassidy. And you are not wrong to love your father. That is normal. It is part of our nature, to love someone. And also in our nature is to protect. Sometimes people that aren't emotionally involved, who are standing on the outside looking in, can see better, they are in a better position to protect those who can't protect themselves. T.J., this is one of those times. Anyone looking at your father could see that he was dangerous to you and your family. He had to be stopped. You needed to be protected."

Not saying a word, the little girl looked to her mother. Sara nodded, because she knew that though she couldn't say the words, James was right. The papers were full of men who thought that they loved their families and killed them to prove it.

Stewart stood up. "Director, it's not as good as the hospital, but it will suffice until she can see a surgeon."

James looked up to him. "Thank you Stewart. Get things ready. The chopper needs to be in the air as soon as Butler arrives."

The two men left them alone. Sara lifted her foot. It was encased on a large bandage boot and sort of looked like a small q-tip. The pills had taken the edge off.

"Thanks for the pills. They help. Did you say Butler was coming?'

"Yes. I need to explain my actions and get out of here. I am persona non grata with the agency right now. I have a villa in Greece that I will be retiring to. Mavin was supposed to deliver the three of you here, unharmed. That was the idea. I didn't know, couldn't know, anyhow- that he would go to the extent that he did. A good agent is dead. I can't change that. But at least the guilty party was punished. I do hope that you and your daughters can forgive me."

Sara looked up at him incredulously. "Are you fucking serious? My family is kidnapped, my daughter shot, I am shot in front of my youngest daughter, Butler is nearly killed in front of both my kids and you hope I can forgive you? Excuse the hell of me, but a cold day in hell is more likely to happen before then!"

He shrugged. "I am sorry that you feel that way. But it had to be proven that it only took one thing to bring the whole operation down."

They both looked at the door when the baying of hounds got loud enough that it was apparent they were right outside the door. The thumping of the helicopter blades overhead had to be the police.

"YOU INSIDE, COME OUT WITH YOUR HANDS UP!"

Sara looked a James. "So what happens now?"

"With any luck, they will listen to Agent Butler and stay put until he can get here. Until then, we will just sit here and share a moment."

"What's he like?"

"Whom? The Prince or Butler?"

"Both..."

"His Highness is intelligent, capable, caring and totally in love with his children, all three of them." James told her pointedly. Then he gave a good chuckle that made his shoulders lift bit. "The same could be said of Butler. But he has no children. That's not saying that he can't or shouldn't have them. Personally, I think he would make a terrific father. Maybe you should talk to him about that."

His phone laying on the table began to vibrate. Picking it up and hitting the send button, James smiles "speak of the devil." He punched a few buttons and hit send. A few seconds later, there was a knock on the door.

As Butler opened it and came in, Sara could see through the opening that they were surrounded by a small army of police and SWAT member. It looked like a major standoff.

Slowly closing the door, he looked over at Sara and felt his heart leap. T.J. was sitting next to James, who was smiling as if he were at a party instead of a kidnapping scene.

Standing and enveloping Butler in a great hug, the older man thumped him hard on the back. "Good to see you alive. I had no idea that Mavin would go over the bend like this."

Butler pushed him away to level a look into his eyes. "Mr. Director, you have some serious explaining to do."

"No Rhett, I don't. I only have to get out of here and leave you to handle clean-up. I just wanted to make sure that you had things in hand. And by the way, talk to Sara here about kids."

With that, he grabbed his phone from the table and threw it on the floor. Before Sara had a chance to think or Butler a chance to react, the room was filled with thick smoke that made their eyes tear and shut.

Blindly feeling for Sara and T.J., Butler grabbed them by the hands, stumbled to the door and flung it open. He pulled the two down to the ground with him and laid flat while the room filled with cops in gas masks. Standard procedure was to throw everyone on the floor, then figure out the good guys from the bad guys when the smoke cleared. In this case it was literal and Agent Riggins identified Butler as the good guy, Sara and T.J. as the victims.

Seconds later, two small choppers were in the air and roaring away. Butler knew that one was probably a hired decoy and the other held the Director and his agents.

As their eyes cleared and they were able to breath, Butler looked at Sara. She was o.k., as was T.J. They both looked worse for wear, but they were O.K. As Sara was out onto an ambulance gurney he looked at Sara "Care to fill in the blanks?"

Chapter 72

As Cassidy was wheeled into recovery, Thompson was at her side. He was careful to stay out of the nurses way, but it was an unspoken understanding that he wasn't leaving her side.

The doctor had left to tell Maria and Amanda that baring any infection, Cassidy would make a full recovery and have full use of her arm.

Thompson called Riggins and told her the report. She informed him of the recovery of the rest of the family and that they were en route to the hospital for Sara's injury repair. It was going to be a long day for the surgeon.

The ride to the hospital was quiet. Sara knew that everything James had told her was in confidence and the back of an ambulance with non-British security and EMT's was not a good place.

It was an awkward silence that filled the ambulance. A Pennsylvania state trooper was in the back with them. Butler had already informed him that Sara could not answer specifics at that time, but a full report from the British Consulate would be forth coming. Butler knew that this was going to get ugly. Not too mention tricky. An attack by a British national on another British national was one thing. But put an attack on two American children at their home in suburban New Jersey, there was going to be hell to pay.

Sara was quietly processing the entire two weeks in her Head. She was starting to get a headache. She looked over at Butler.

"Rhett?"

His turned red. "I thought you might catch that."

"Care to explain?" She was becoming amused by his discomfort

"My mother was fascinated with "Gone with the Wind". She even named our small house and property "Tara".

"Oh, she didn't?" Despite her pain, she started to laugh out loud.

T.J. looked confused "What's so funny?"

Holding her daughter's hand she tried to get her laughter in check. "Sweety, in the movie Gone With The Wind, there is a character named "Rhett Butler". It's seems that Mr. Butler's mother has a bit of an obsession."

Butler smiled slightly. "Imagine growing up hearing people saying they don't give a damn. Curse of my life. But since I love my mother, despite her quirkiness, I never changed it."

"Oh. that is so sweet."

He looked at Riggins and the State Trooper. "If this ever gets out, I will make sure that going to the loo will become very adventurous for you.

They both chuckled and shook their heads. Riggins burst out laughing "Frankly my dear...."

Butler held up a finger "Don't finish that." he threatened

The silence lasted for a second, then everyone in the ambulance burst out laughing. It was on a good note that they pulled into the hospital.

Epilogue

By the time Sara's foot had been put back together- a grueling four hours in surgery then another hour casting it, all the blanks were filled in.

Sara related to him what James had told her. That Mavin had been instructed to fetch Sara and the girls. That the killing of the two techs and Tim had all been Mavin's doing. James had wanted a bloodless abduction and if Mavin had followed the plans, it would have gone off that way. But then plans of mice and men....

Butler got on the phone to give Director Laraby a heads up about the plan. She in turn informed him that the younger Prince was under house arrest and that he would probably be taking a long vacation.

Butler knew that it was an unspoken death sentence. Not that it wasn't expected. A traitor came in many forms. This was just one more. Ambition did strange things to people and just because you have a title doesn't make you any different than the rest of the world. Or maybe it did, because it was on such a larger scale. Some people killed for money, some for love or some just to get more of something they imagine will make them bigger and better. When it came to Royals, they stood to inherit a world. Just went to prove the saying, power corrupts, but absolute power corrupts absolutely.

He looked at his closed phone in his hands then looked at the closed door to Sara's room.

The surgeon said that she would be in a cast for at least a week, then suture removal and another cast for a couple of months. Cassidy was going to make a full recovery and Butler felt absolutely useless. Never in his entire career had anyone got the drop on him, not even when he was a rookie. Looking up at the ceiling and leaning back against the wall, he thought of what to do next. He was in love with Sara Cohen. Attorney, divorced mother of two and a Royal. There was no way they could make this work.

Sara and Cassidy shared a room that had been overloaded with flowers and stuffed animals. One delivery was especially noticeable. the stuffed animal was the biggest that they had ever seen. It was accompanied by a note that said "Always out there to protect you." Sara knew it was from James. She said a prayer for him that he lived long and enjoyed his retirement. Even though he had been a part of all this mess, he had done it with the best of intentions.

They were the lead story on every network. reporters had mobbed the hospital and were trying their best to get in. Sara's father got to the hospital just after Sara came out of casting. Her brother called to say that their houses had been converged on by the press and to stay away as long as possible. Maria and Amanda had refused to leave them once they came out of recovery. Sleeper chairs were brought in for them. A chair had also been brought in for T.J., but she simply curled up along side her mother and fell asleep.

It got late by the time everyone had fallen asleep. Everyone except for Sara.

She lay on the bed, her foot propped up on a mountain of pillows. With T.J. tucked contentedly under her arm. she looked over at Cassidy who was already asleep and lightly snoring. Her mother and sister were also sleeping, the reclining chairs obviously more comfortable than they looked.

For the first time, Sara let herself think about Butler. A small smile crept across her face when she remembered his first name. It was sweet, that he cared enough about his mother not to change it. Her heart took a dip when she thought about him. She barely knew the man and she knew that she was more in love with him than she had ever been with anyone else. It was like a fist around her heart, the pressure was almost painful.

She also knew that they couldn't make it work. There were too many obstacles And the more she thought about the obstacles, the more she realized that they weren't as insurmountable as she thought. All it was going to take was a bit of compromise and adaptation. Gently she eased out from under T.J. and reached for her purse. Pulling out her PDA, she accessed her phone.

The troopers and sheriff's deputies had been released with official "Thank's" and letters of commendation that would be forth coming from the Brits. An official story that the British national that had been abducted was Cathy Marshall, a member of Parliament that had been vacationing in the States and had been staying with Sara and her family. Cathy had been called and told that she was the cover story and that at some later date she would be filled in to the small details. Knowing Sara the way she did, she trusted her and went along with the story. Since she was on holiday, it was a cover story that worked well.

Butler, Riggins and the rest of the team were ordered back to London for debriefing. An entire new team had been put into place, including the computer techs.

The agent in the room with Sara and her girls was a nice woman. Her name was Agent Kindrick and she had been with MI-6 for less than five years. She got a good laugh out of it when T.J told her that she looked like her kindergarten teacher.

With a conspiratorial wink, she told the little girl that it was part of her cover, to put people at ease. It didn't go unnoticed by Sara that the woman carried a nine millimeter under her coat and she caught a glimpse of a small gun strapped to her ankle. The woman might look domesticated, but Sara was certain that they were in good and capable hands.

Maria and Amanda left the next morning. Reports coming back from Phil gave every indication that it was going to be a hung jury, so Amanda and Sara would be going at it again. The little sister wanted to get home to prepare, while Maria wanted to get Barry home and get things ready for two injured people who were going to need extra care when they got there. They took T.J. home with them, just so that she would start her own recovery from the trauma she had experienced. Maria knew the littlest internalized things. She also had an easier time talking to her "gamma" and "pop-pop" than to her mother. Sara was a good mother and a caring person, but sometimes it was just easier talking to someone who you loved but wasn't so high energy .

After everyone had cleared out of the room, it was just Sara and Cassidy. The agent had posted outside of the room while the agent outside of the room went with T.J. Sara knew that it would be like this for a few days, then things would settle down and go back to as before. She was absently watching a talk show and working on her notes when Cassidy turned the t.v. off. Sara looked over at her and put the PDA down. *Here it comes* she thought.

"Mom. I have a few questions. Number one, who is Butler?"

Sara sat up as best as she could and taking a deep breath, she gave a thought as to how much the kids needed to know.

"Butler is an MI-6 agent. During his work here, he uncovered a plot to unite the Bloods and a British Muslim gang here in the U.S. Part of the merger was to take me and my family out. Butler was sent to protect us until our own CIA could take them out.

"But the news said that Aunt Cathy...."

Sara held up a hand to interrupt her "Sweety, how many times have you heard Uncle Pete tell us about the government trying to keep gang activity on the D.L? This is one of those times. If the general public knows the extent that gangs network, who would sleep at night? Who would be in office? No one wants to acknowledge that there is a gang war going on."

"So that guy who shot me, he is or was a Muslim?'

"Yeah. He was. But he's dead now."

"Will there be others like him?"

"I don't think so. Our people and MI-6 proved that it is too dangerous for them to try to operate over here right now. We'll have an agent for a few days, maybe even a week, but after that, I think things will die down enough so that we can let them go."

"Mom. Do you believe in love at first sight?"

Sara looked at her daughter in shock and surprise. She raised her eyebrow and wondered exactly how observant her daughter was. "Yes, as a matter of fact I do. Why?"

"I saw the way you looked at Butler, when he said that he would die trying to protect us. The way you looked at him is the same way that Gamma looks at Pop-pop, and the way that Aunt Manda looks at Uncle Phil. I just wanted to tell you that if you love Butler, I won't be mad at you. I know Daddy wasn't the best person for us. I heard the police talking about how he kidnapped you and I think I agree with Gamma- he should be taken outside and shot."

Sara was shocked. Despite everything her ex-husband had done, she had made sure that she hadn't bad mouthed him to the girls. She wanted them to make their own decision, come to their own conclusions about their father. A weight lifted off of her shoulders. She had wondered what would happen when this day came, and now she knew.

Holding hands across the space between the hospital beds they smiled at each other. Every time Sara looked at Cassidy, she marveled at how beautiful she was and at how fast she was growing.

"I'm both happy and sad that you feel that way. I really tried to shield you girls from the unpleasantness that is life. I wish I had done better. But I am happy that I've done well enough that you seem to have your head on straight where your father is concerned. But this thing with Butler, it's complicated and it's going to take time. All right?"

She nodded and leaned in for a hug. They both said "ow" at the same time as they bumped each others wounds. Sara leaned back and let out a sigh.

"Baby, I am so sorry that you got shot."

Cassidy let out a snort "Put that into your book of things you never thought that you would have to tell your children."

"Yeah. Right up there with "Stop licking the cat."

"Aw. Come on. I was four and the cat was doing it. I just wanted to see how it felt."

"And...."

"I didn't like it too much."

"As I recall, the cat wasn't too fond of it, either."

It had been a short flight from Newark to London. They all flew commercial to save money. It struck Butler as almost funny that the movies always depicted the Team as highly funded, larger than life. Those movies never showed them getting receipts, grocery shopping or having a bad case of the flu

He got out of the cab in front of his townhouse and paid the driver. She tried to hand Butler his changed, but he waived her off. Might as well make someone happy. He slowly went up the stairs, dreading when he would have to go in.

He slid the key into the lock and turned the knob. Shoving the door open he walked in and turned on the lights. It was exactly as they had left it that day when they went on holiday. The only difference was the mail in the catch basket attached to the door. Droping his duffel bag on the floor by the umbrella stand, he gathered the mail out of the basket and started to sort through it. After he made two neat piles on the hallway table, he found his thoughts going to Sara. Her smile. Her hair color. Her laugh. Her kids. Looking up at the wall behind the table, his eyes were met with his wedding picture. Katey had been a beautiful bride. Her long thin strapless dress, the white roses of her buquet. She had been blond, beautiful and intelligent. He missed her so much.

But in his heart, he knew she was gone and he was in love with Sara Cohen. He made his way to the kitchen and absently opened the fridge. Nothing to eat. He was going to have to do some shopping. He shut the fridge and went to stairs. He stopped at the bottom. He remembered carrying Katey up the stairs when they got back from the reception. It had taken them a few minutes-he couldn't stop kissing her with every step. It didn't matter that they had lived together for five years before finally taking the plunge. There was something about taking vows that had made it all seem so new.

Walking into their bedroom, he could still see Katey waking up and looking at him, smiling, her faced still creased from the sheets. It was like a wave, engulfing him. He staggered over to the bed and cried. The deep sobs wracking his body. He had not allowed himself to grieve like this. He let himself lay down on the bed, clutching a pillow to stifle the howl that was rising in his chest. She was gone and there was nothing left except the memories. He could still smell her perfume lingering in the air, but not on the bedding. Her clothes were still in the drawers and the closet. All the plans that they had made were laid to waste in the snow that had taken Katey's life.

It was dark by the time the tears stopped. Butler was drained and felt like a wrung out rag when he stood up. As he turned on the lights, he saw an envelope sticking out from under the phone. It was addressed to him.

He sat down on the bed and tore it open. It was James' handwriting.

Rhett,

If everything thing has gone as planned, you are in your room getting ready for your debriefing.

Nothing happened that I didn't orchestrate. From the DNA theft to Laraby's promotion. Remember, the easiest way to get someone to do what you want is to make them think that it s their idea. And by making Laraby look like a baracuda, i could go out in disgrace and never be bothered by MI-6 again. I have enough dirt on people that I'm safe, but enough of a reputation for integrity that I'm not a threat.

Rhett, my friend, this room is depressing and you need to move on. Katey was a lovely girl, but I knew her before you did. She would hate the shrine that you have turned this house into. Do yourself a favor, and that of Katey's memory and pack up her things and give them away. Life is short and there is someone in the States that Katey would have loved, and would love for you to be with.

James

Butler closed the letter and let his head fall against the wood headboard. His thoughts went back to Sara. He looked at the picture montage on the opposite wall. Katey had spent hours framing and hanging the pictures. She looked so happy. James had been right. She would really be mad at him for this. They had talked about it, if one of them outlived the other. They had both silently assumed that he would be the one to die first, probably when they were still young. Katey had promised him that she would move on, love again and not hang on to what they had, but cherish it as a bright memory. Katey had been the love of his life. And now he owed it to her to keep the promise, to go on and learn to love again.

Butler and the rest of the Team sat around the conference table, each with a computer in front of them. They would each write their statements as they saw things, then match them up to what the cameras had recorded then file their reports. Each one of the reports would be scrutinized. The analysts would pour over each report, pick it apart and figure out how they screwed up and how to not let it happen again.

Four dead, one injured, one Director either rogue or damned brilliant-and missing. And all Butler could think about was Sara.

He had kept tabs on her and the girls. He had watched the news reports, read the surveillance reports and watched her and Cassidy in the hospital from the camera that was hidden in the t.v. monitor. and all he wanted to do was be with her. London was too far away. He looked away from his computer and saw Riggins staring at him. A sly grin came to her face and she stood up and walked over to him. Sitting on the corner of the table, she pretended to examine her nails.

"You know, there is a plane at Heathrow leaving every hour for New York. And New York is only forty five minutes from a cute little house in New Jersey with a lady barrister, two cute kids and a cat,"

"And your point is?"

"Why Mistah Butler" she said in a mock southern accent "I do declare, you should be in that beast and heading out to see that thar Yankee. Seriously (she dropped the accent). Go get her. You are in love with her and I know she's in love with you. Kitridge says that you are all she gets happy about. It's almost nauseating."

The door to the room opened and Director Laraby came in alone and shut the door behind her. Pulling out the closest unoccupied chair, she sat down and opened a file she brought in with her.

"I've read your reports and followed your notes. Based on intel that we have from various sources and your records, you are all to return to the Team, but you will be posted in different locations. It is the feeling of the analyst's that perhaps a change of venue would help prevent such errors in judgment and disregard for protocol in the future. You may all leave for the day. You will receive your new assignments in the morning. Mr. Butler, a word if you don't mind.

As the other agents filed out, Riggins gave him a thumbs up before she went through the door. It gave him a boost that his flagging spirit needed.

After they had all left and the door was shut, Laraby closed the folder and pushed it away. She pulled off her glasses and rubbed the bridge of her nose. Butler knew she wore the glasses for reading, a definite sign that they were all getting older.

"Butler...when James pulled you for this case, I was against it, and it appears with good reason. I felt that you weren't ready to be back in the field. You got sloppy. Your orders were to rescue Miss Cohen and if she proved to be a liability, take her out. Miss Cohen was not a liability as long as she was in the dark about her identity. Since you are familiar with the persons of interest in this case, it would be most practical for you to go back and make it look like a tragic accident. I'm not telling you how to do your job, Butler. I'm just telling you that a story for the papers has already been written about the tragic fire that claimed the life of Prosecutor Cohen and her family."

Butler's blood ran cold.

As they left the hospital three days later, the press had been neatly avoided by their laundry truck exit. Cassidy had thought it was great fun playing "Spy Escape" as she called it. Sara was just glad to have avoided the barrage of reporters and microphones that would be shoved in her face. The laundry truck stopped a couple of blocks away where they were met by her parents and T.J. It was a quick get away in case one of the cagier reporters figured out the ruse.

As they pulled into their driveway, with the exception of the family cars, it was blissfully empty. Agent Kitridge had been in a car that followed closely behind. Since Sara and Cassidy weren't scheduled to be discharged for another day, the press hadn't been camped out for the last two day, much to the entire neighborhoods relief.

As they went in, another agent was already in the kitchen making coffee and putting out a plate of deserts. And even though it was just family in the house, it was over crowded. Shaking her head, Sara gave a rueful smile. Even just family was a small army. The cacaphoney of noise was accented by various cell phones ringing and the kids "ooing" and "awing" over Cassidy's story of getting shot.

Pete came over to where she was sitting, knelt to her level and hugged her tightly "Dammit woman. Don't you ever do that to me again. My old heart can only take so much."

Sara craned her neck as best she could to look at the crowd. "I expected Amanda to be here."

He shook his head. "She was for about a minute. The jury came back just before you guys pulled into the driveway. I'm surprised you didn't see her car pass you."

"Are you shitting me? I should be there. Come on, let me up- I can still make an appearance."

Feeling her mother's hands on her shoulders halted her attempt to stand. "Sit your ass down and don't even think about it. You have been shot, kidnapped and had surgery. And unless you want me to get that agent over there to cuff you to the bed, you will NOT move from this house for at least forty eight hours."

Maria didn't use that tone of voice very often, but when she did everyone knew not to mess with her.

Sara was no exception nor was she a fool. Resigning herself to the situation she looked up at her mother "Yes Momma." She knew who was in charge and at that moment it wasn't her.

Amanda looked at her watch as she hurried out of the parking garage. It had helped that the jury had come back after the morning rush hour. As she climbed the steps to the courthouse, she could see Hakiem waiting for her at the entrance by the sheriff's desk. He looked calm and relaxed. As she got closer, he smiled at her. It wasn't the smile that made a shiver run down Amanda's spine. It was the look in his eye, sort of the wolf looking at a piece of meat. And while she was no stranger to appreciative looks from men, there was something in this man's eyes that made her wary.

"Good morning, Hakiem. Shall we go in?"

Placing her brief case on the conveyor belt so that it could be scanned, she walked through the metal detector, closely followed by her client. He was so close to her that she could smell his after shave. It surprised her that she found it very pleasant and provocative. The deputy handed her the briefcase and they silently went to the elevator. Amanda looked around then back at the young man. "No posse today?"

As the doors closed and he pressed the button he smiled down at her again, the same smile that made her heart flinch. "They already went up. I remember you saying that all of us in the elevator together made you a little claustrophobic. I thought that it would be better this way."

She cocked an eyebrow at him and smiled. "Well, thank you very much. That was very considerate of you." He looked devastatingly handsome. Another time, another place, she would have given him a shot at the title as "The Best She Ever Had". But this was not the time, nor the place nor the person. It must be the whole Bad Boy thing. He oozed charm, energy and danger. At that moment, she could understand why some women were willing to throw away everything for a man.

The doors slid open and they stepped out and were met by Hakiem's "friends". On one hand, Amanda was sure that she would have to be in a bullet proof room to be safer, on the other hand-she felt almost dirty.

Enmass, they went into the court room and made their way to the Defendant's table. Phil was already seated and waiting. He looked confident, but Amanda could see the twinge of nervousness around his eyes. Phil had made a good argument, but Amanda's had been more convincing, or compelling and they all knew it.

There was almost no wait until the judge was seated and the t.v. monitor was turned on to reflect the jurors filing in to a separate room. Even now, no one was taking any chances. As the courtroom was brought to order, Amanda noticed that none of the jurors were looking in the direction of the camera. She wasn't sure if this was good or not. Not making eye contact had been a small hinderance during the trial. Now during the verdict reading, it was just damn unnerving.

The judge waited while the court stenographer opened the file on her computer. When she signaled the judge that she was ready, he looked over at the camera that the jury would be seeing on their monitor..

"I understand that you have reached a verdict?"

Three people stood up and each handed the deputy a separate piece of paper. The deputy opened the door and the papers would be handed off to another deputy who would walk the papers to the judge. A couple of minutes later, the deputy entered the court room and handed the papers to the judge. The judge read them and looking at the camera he folded the papers. "So say you all?" a loud chorus of "yes" came from the monitor.

The judge looked over at Hakiem. No matter how the jury decided, this was not going to be pretty. He gathered himself mentally and physically checked for the gun that he kept at his waist under his robes. One could never be too careful. "The defendant will rise."

Amanda and Hakiem stood. She looking professional and pensive, he was looking as cool as a cucumber.

The judge unfolded the paper again. Not pretty. "Due to the circumstances requiring the jury anonymity, I will be reading the verdict. Are there any objections?"

Both Phil and Amanda shook their heads. "No your Honor" was echoed in unison. She choked back a small smile-they sounded as if they had rehearsed it.

Clearing his throat, the judge began reading from the paper "In the case of the State of New Jersey versus Hakiem Borden, this jury finds you Not guilty of all charges. You are free to go and all bail monies returned. This court thanks the jurists for their time and they are excused, this court is now in recess."

The gallery erupted in a roar. Some were happy and jubilant, while some were screaming that an injustice had been done. Amanda turned to congratulate Hakiem when she felt something push past her so hard that she was momentarily unbalanced. As she reached out to Hakiem to steady herself, she looked up in time to see a knife sticking out of his neck, blood spurting in a high arc from his jugular vein. For a split second there was silence. Then a scream shattered the silence and pandamonium broke out. As Hakiem fell onto Amanda, she grabbed under his shoulders to roll him and lay him flat in one smooth move. While she tried to stop the flow of blood from his neck with her hands, it showered onto her, soaking into her blouse. Deputies were pulling guns, locking down the courtroom and getting the judge out safely, all at the same time.

The prime directive of stab wounds in first care was to leave the knife in the wound, Amanda knew that in order to stop the bleeding, it would have to come out. She handed it to the deputy who had magically appeared with a first aid kit in his hand. She looked up at the deputy and said *"evidence"* as she watched him nod. At least he had the professional presence of mind to know what she was talking about. She may be for the defense, but she was still married to the State's chief prosecutor.

SWAT had already been standing by as a "just in case" measure. They had already come in and everyone in the gallery- man, woman and child, it didn't matter- was face down on the floor. The EMT's were escorted in and took over holding pressure on Hakiem's neck. They couldn't hold pressure too tight or they would strangle him. On the other hand, if they didn't hold it tight enough, it would start bleeding again. Three deputies and one of the EMT's loaded him onto the stretcher while the paramedics started I.V's and put an oxygen mask on him. Everything was being done so fast that Amanda was amazed.

The irony hit her as they were wheeling him out of the court room. Five minutes before people in this courtroom had wanted to see him die, now some of those very people could be seen praying for him. Amanda knew that some of those prayers weren't for his recovery, but for his demise. The deputy who had come up with the first aid kit touched her arm. "Are you alright, ma'am?" She nodded.

"Yeah, thanks. Did they get the stabber?" Jerking his head toward a small crowd of cops on the floor "Oh, yeah. It was the witness who said it was his kid that got killed."

Shaking her head, Amanda was not surprised. "My question is how did he get that in here?"

The deputy, Labrano, held up the clear plastic evidence bag for her to see. "It's one of those ceramic knives that you can get at the chef's store. It doesn't set off the metal detectors and this one is so small that he could have tucked it anywhere and the guys downstairs wouldn't have felt it when they patted him down. You're just lucky the guy went after your client and not you."

That thought hadn't occurred to her. But now that it did, she felt her heart almost stop. It shocked her enough, stunned her to sudden silence and no movement. Labrano reached out a hand to get her attention. The blood had absolutely drained from her face. "Ms. Cohen, I didn't mean to scare you. Are you alright?"

Nodding blindly, she looked down at her hands still covered in Hakiem's blood. And suddenly it was all too much. Sara getting kidnapped twice, Cassidy getting shot, the standoff in the woods and her sister's rescue. Now this. It was all too much. She turned and looked at Phil. The witness, Ronald Townsend, now the attempted- murderer was being read his rights.

She had to get out of there. Get home. With that thought and drive in mind, she grabbed her purse and walked out of the courtroom, through the judge's chambers, down the back stairs and to her car. Hands bloody, clothes beginning to reek from the coppery smelling blood, past the gathering reporters. She didn't care. She needed her family.

Sara looked around the house. It was filled from top to bottom with flowers, stuffed animals, candy and food baskets. There wasn't an inch of flat surface that wasn't occupied by something from a well wisher.

T.J. was showing Cassidy the toys that she had received as well as the cards that had been addressed to her. Then she took her sister on a tour of all the stuff that had been sent to both of them and then to stuff just for Cassidy. It was like Christmas in June. Sara's head began to spin. This was way too much.

The agent brought out the coffee on a tray and handed it to her. "Good day, Ma'am. I am Agent Hopkins. I'll be leaving as soon as Agent Kitridge here says so. I asked your mother about most of the baskets. We sent the perishable fruits to the homeless shelter. The rest, your mother thought you would get a kick out of the enormity of it."

Sara sipped the coffee and looked at Hopkins over the rim. "My mother is a sadist."

Maria walked in and laughed. "I sure am. I am taking great pleasure in the fact that you have to write a thank you note to each one of these people."

Sara grunted "Yeah right. I don't think so. The girls, yes-me...Uh, I don't think so."

The older woman lightly slapped her hand "You most certainly will. I raised you better than that. Phil says he can handle your case load for a few days, that gives you a four day weekend. Since you have me, Dad and Agent Kitridge here to handle things, you have no excuse. Isn't that right Agent Kitridge?"

She shrugged at Sara "Sorry Ma'am, but your mother does have a point." The agent could barely hide her smile.

"It's a conspiracy, I tell you." She glared at her mother "You did this on purpose didn't you. You know how much I love writing those things."

Maria laughed. "Tell you what, Spanky Pants, I'll go through the cards, baskets and everything else. I will even separate the ones that need a thank you and the ones that don't. I will go as far as going out to buy the stamps and address the ones that I can. I will do all of that if you go upstairs and rest. Is that a good compromise? And by rest, I do not mean work on one of your cases."

Even as her mind jumped to her PDA and her brief case, Sara felt the fatigue set in. She didn't realize how tired she was. Looking over at Cassidy, the child was already asleep on the couch and Kitridge was pulling a light blanket up to the child's chin.

Nodding, she got up on her crutches and headed for the stairs. She had been practicing using the metal crutches at the hospital and was rapidly becoming a pro at it. She got to the stairs and hopped up them on one leg.

"Please be careful" her mother called after her. A person would think she was fourteen instead of forty.

Getting to her room presented no problem, but negotiating the cast around the small bathroom and not hitting it against the wall or the sink was something else. She finished and flushed, dropped her crutch on the floor, bent down to pick it up and hit her head on the sink. While she was holding her head, she banged her foot on the toilet and cursed out loud at the pain that shot up her leg.

It was then that she saw the brick of C-4 attached to the underside of sink. The bright flash of light cut off the warning she tried to get out.